W9-BFX-427

Behind the masks

The others had finished hiding their cards and were complacently sipping wine. They were smiling at me, apparently friendly: Zena, Manny, and Joe, the glamorous people next door, who really did seem to like me after all, forgiving me for this afternoon, including me in their game.

Only right now, they were a hairy spider-lady; a fish-man with a long, razor-sharp horn growing out of his head; and a flying octopus with claws. And they would happily kill me to get the smiling pink Piggy in my hand. . . .

❌ ❌ ❌ ❌ ❌

FIREBIRD
WHERE FANTASY TAKES FLIGHT™

INTERSTELLAR PIG

Books by William Sleator:

The Beasties

The Boxes

The Boy Who Reversed Himself

Dangerous Wishes

The Duplicate

The Green Futures of Tycho

House of Stairs

Interstellar Pig

Into the Dream

Marco's Millions

The Night the Heads Came

Oddballs

Others See Us

Parasite Pig

Rewind

Singularity

The Spirit House

Strange Attractors

INTERSTELLAR PIG

WILLIAM SLEATOR

FIREBIRD

AN IMPRINT OF PENGUIN GROUP (USA) INC.

FIREBIRD
Published by Penguin Group
Penguin Group (USA) Inc.,
345 Hudson Street, New York, New York 10014, U.S.A.
Penguin Books Ltd, 80 Strand, London WC2R ORL, England
Penguin Books Australia Ltd, 250 Camberwell Road,
Camberwell, Victoria 3124, Australia
Penguin Books Canada Ltd, 10 Alcorn Avenue, Toronto, Ontario, Canada M4V 3B2
Penguin Books (N.Z.) Ltd, 182-190 Wairau Road, Auckland 10, New Zealand

First published in the United States of America by E. P. Dutton, 1984
Published by Puffin Books, 1995
Published by Firebird, an imprint of Penguin Group (USA) Inc., 2004

9 10 8

THE LIBRARY OF CONGRESS HAS CATALOGED THE DUTTON EDITION AS FOLLOWS:
Sleator, William.
Interstellar pig.
Summary: Barney's boring seaside vacation suddenly becomes more interesting when
the cottage next door is occupied by three exotic neighbors
who are addicted to a game they call Interstellar Pig.
[1. Science fiction.] I. Title.
PZ7.S6313Ik 1984 [Fic] 84-4132 ISBN 0-525-44098-4

ISBN 0-14-037595-3

Printed in the United States of America

This book is dedicated to my parents, Esther and Bill Sleator. Though a doctor and a scientist, with similar expectations for me, they bore my decision to make a living as a writer with extraordinary fortitude—and have even, at times, encouraged me.

1

"I'm telling you, there's more history to this house than any other place on Indian Neck, and that's the truth," Ted Martin said, and took a long swallow of beer. He had just finished installing an outside shower, and his forehead was streaked with grime.

"How fascinating," Mom said politely. She was rinsing glasses at the sink. I knew she wasn't very interested in Ted, who had no social importance.

"What kind of history?" asked my father. Ted was the caretaker of the beach house we were renting for two weeks in July. We had been there for one week already, and had heard nothing unusual about the house.

"This was a Captain Latham's house. I heard there was even an article written about the tragedy here." Ted chuckled. "They even used to say it was haunted."

1

"Haunted?" I asked him. "What do you mean?" I had been hovering in the doorway in my usual indecisive way, but now I took a couple of eager steps into the kitchen. I had not been enjoying this vacation on the beach. The house was far from the village. There didn't seem to be any other kids my age—which was sixteen—in the area. We were surrounded by nature reserves, and I wasn't big on nature. I wouldn't even be able to go home with a tan, since I can't lie in the sun for fifteen minutes without burning miserably. A supposedly haunted house might be a welcome diversion from the science fiction books I had been reading.

"What do you mean, haunted?" I asked Ted again. "What kind of tragedy?"

"Captain Latham had a trading ship in the last century, out of the harbor here. Dunstable was almost as important a port as Boston, in the early days, you know. Used to sail from here to China and places." Ted paused to make sure this important piece of special information would be fully appreciated. "He had a younger brother, this Captain Latham. He was a sailor on Captain Latham's ship. Never was too bright. And after what happened, his mind went completely. Off the deep end, you know. The captain kept him locked in the front bedroom here for twenty years."

This was getting really interesting—I slept in the front bedroom.

"After *what* happened?" I said.

Ted took another long, slow swallow, then studied the label on the beer bottle approvingly. "Good stuff," he said. "Where'd you pick it up?"

"In Boston," said Dad.

2

"First-rate suds," Ted said. "Can't get it around here."

"Come on, tell us about this tragedy," I said, really curious now.

"Well, Captain Latham's ship was out in the South Pacific somewhere, and they picked up this shipwrecked sailor. Nothing left of *his* ship but the timber he was floating on. There wasn't much room on those traders, you know, and the guy they rescued had to bunk down with somebody else. The captain's brother got him. The next morning the stranger was dead. Kind of too bad, after he got out of his shipwreck alive. Strangled. Ever see somebody who was strangled? Red marks on the throat and the eyes popping out and the tongue all black and swollen and—"

"No. I never have," Mom said, putting a hand on her pink neck.

"Well, it was the captain's brother that killed him, everybody could see that. Didn't even try to deny it. Must have been a little embarrassing for the captain."

"They were drinking and had a fight, I suppose," Dad said, trying to prod Ted along.

"No drinking, no fight. The brother just strangled him. Quietly."

"But there must have been some reason," I said, sitting down across from Ted.

"I told you, the brother never was too bright. They had a kind of trial, like they did on those ships, and they asked him why. And he just raved a lot of nonsense, nobody could get any sense out of him. All about the stranger being the Devil, crazy stuff like that. Brother must have just had a bad dream, and didn't know what he was doing, that's the only explanation they could come up

3

with. So Captain Latham, he was in a real dilemma, since he had to see that justice was done. But he couldn't really stomach hanging his own brother. So he sentenced him to be keelhauled."

"What's that?" I asked.

"They tie a rope to him. And they tie the other end of the rope to the back of the ship. Then they toss the guy off the *front* of the ship. So you know what happens then?" Ted sat up in his chair and leaned forward with enthusiasm.

"Go on," I said impatiently. "What?"

"He gets dragged underneath the ship, for the whole length of the ship. Dragged across all the sharp jagged barnacles there. The brother was sliced up real bad. Most of the time a man drowns, since he's under the water for a while. But sometimes they don't drown. There's always that chance. That's why the captain preferred keelhauling his brother to hanging him." Ted paused to finish his beer.

"And he didn't drown, is that it?" I said. "The captain and his brother were lucky in the end?"

"That depends. He was alive, all right, when they pulled him out. But he was under there so long without breathing that he got permanent brain damage. Lack of oxygen to the brain cells or something. He was a raving lunatic from then on. Never said another sensible word in his life, locked up in the front bedroom here. Didn't do nothing but mew like a sick cat and claw the walls. You can still see the scratch marks all around the windows."

"Whose car is that coming up the road?" Mom asked. She was usually a little suspicious of strangers and tended to avoid them until she was sure of their reputation.

Ted turned slowly to glance through the window be-

4

hind his chair. "Oh, that must be *them,* the ones who rented the cottage next door. They were supposed to show up an hour or so ago." He chuckled and shook his head. "This here's the place they wanted, but they were too late. Already rented it to you folks. Man, were they ever disappointed. Never heard anybody get so upset about a summer rental. They even tried to bribe me, but I have my ethics. And they wouldn't take it for August, it had to be *now.* Tried to tell them the cinder-block cottage had a better view, and finally they took it."

"I hope you made sure they had proper references," Mom said. "That cottage is so close."

"Sure, sure," Ted said lightly. "But man, I thought I was gonna hear grown men weep when I wouldn't let them have this place. Just didn't make sense the way—"

"Well, thanks for the shower, Ted," Dad said, standing up and extending his hand.

"Guess I better be heading next door," Ted said, rising and making a brief salute. "Thanks for the beer."

I followed him out of the kitchen. I had noticed the scratch marks around the windows of my room, and I was more curious than ever now. "But is that the whole story?" I asked him. "They never found out why he killed the sailor? Nobody knows why he made the scratch marks, or what they mean? How long ago was it? Was he really there for twenty years?"

"Hey, don't you ever stop asking questions, kid?" Ted said, suddenly in a hurry. "I got to see to the new tenants."

"What about that article you said was written about this place? Do you know the name of it, or the author or anything?"

He shrugged and lifted his hands. "Never read it. Somebody just told me about it once. Got to take care of your new neighbors now. Don't want them making another fuss. Never *heard* three people so upset about not getting a summer place, and at the last minute, too. Don't they know places on the beach get taken way ahead? They were lucky to get the cottage when they wanted it. Kinda nutty themselves, if you ask me." He let the screen door slam behind him and loped across the wooden porch.

I waited a moment. Then, opening and shutting the door quietly, so I wouldn't be noticed, I stepped outside.

2

The old gray shingled house we were renting sat on the top of a hill and faced directly out toward the small island about a mile offshore. A fat orange sun was sinking behind the island trees, and restless scribbles of gold danced over the dark water. A mockingbird warbled aggressively from a stunted pine that swayed in the evening wind.

A little gravel road sloped steeply down our scrubby front lawn and wandered off toward a small private beach, several hundred yards to the right. The view was almost perfect, for we were very isolated—the hill the captain had built his house on was the only solid land in the midst of a velvety green salt marsh, on which no houses could be built. Unfortunately, Ted's family had added another house to the top of the hill, to increase the income from their property—a squat cinder-block cube painted a revolting shade of pink, only ten yards to our right. I kept out of sight behind one of the pillars of our porch and watched a woman and two men emerge from the purple Volkswagen convertible parked between the houses.

"God, I thought we'd be in that brutal traffic all night!" the woman cried, flinging her long arms above her head in an impatient, almost violent gesture. Then she saw Ted, and her manner suddenly became demure. "Ted? You must be Ted. Thank you so much for waiting for us," she said, taking his hand. "The voyage took much longer than we thought it would." She was a little shorter than Ted, with a thick mane of black hair. She wore a halter top and denim cutoffs, an outfit that showed her spectacular figure to great advantage. Ted, who had been so talkative a moment before, now seemed tongue-tied as he stared at her.

"Cars were expiring all around us," the woman went on. "If that had happened to ours, I think I might have just left it there and hitchhiked." She smiled sweetly up at Ted.

"You probably wouldn't have had much trouble getting a ride," Ted said.

"Nice domain you got here, Ted," said the man with the brown mustache. "A prime piece of domain, no doubt about it. Prime."

"Well, we do try to take good care of it," Ted said, sounding pleased with himself.

"Our little *logement* does seem to have a better view, just like you told us," said the other man, who had a blond beard. "Even though it's not quite as picturesque as the captain's house."

"The captain? How'd you know the story about the

captain?" Ted demanded, as though the house's history were his own personal property. "*I* didn't say anything about it over the phone."

"Oh, no one told us any kind of *story* about it," the woman quickly explained, with a glance at the blond man, who pressed his lips together. "We don't know any story. That's just what the agent called it—the captain's house, whatever that means." She turned toward our house, and I squeezed back behind the pillar. "But it did make us a trifle curious. And you seem like such an accommodating person, Ted." She smiled at him again, and her voice took on a husky, cajoling quality. "And I was just wondering . . . if those people didn't arrive yet, do you think you could guide us around inside? We'd be so engrossed. I'm sure you've taken wonderful care of it."

"They've been here for a week," Ted said. "Much as I'd enjoy showing it, I don't think they want company now. But there are some things I should tell you about your place. . . ." His voice faded as he moved with them toward the front door of their house. I went quietly back inside.

The two windows in our dark, pine-paneled dining room faced directly toward the cement patio in front of the cinder-block cottage. Mom and Dad sat at the ends of the table, and I sat on the side, opposite the windows. We all had a perfect view when the neighbors emerged in their swimsuits with a tray of bottles and glasses.

Mom was the first to look away from them. "Why, Barney, you haven't even touched your burger," she said.

I quickly took a bite. But I also kept watching. It wasn't just that all three of the neighbors had the bodies of athletes. There was also a casual, animal grace to their move-

9

ments that attracted the eye simply because it was so unusual. I knew they were just three people—but somehow I felt as though I were watching three lions.

"That's really an adorable bikini she's wearing, don't you think?" Mom said. "Only the poor dear should know better than to show herself in something that skimpy at her age. She just doesn't have the figure for it anymore."

I choked on a sip of milk, and Dad gave Mom a puzzled glance. The woman's figure was as flawless as any movie star's. "Her figure looks all right to me," Dad said, making a gross understatement.

"It's especially unflattering on her in comparison to those two striking young men," Mom said, as though she hadn't heard him. "They could be models or something."

"Models?" Dad said. "Those ordinary-looking guys? They're a little on the puny side if you ask me."

I had to laugh. Mom and Dad, who were middle-aged and out of shape, were trying to rationalize their way out of being compared unfavorably to these perfect physical specimens. It seemed rather childish.

"I wonder what it is they see in her," Mom said. "Maybe she has money. That would explain it." The idea seemed to satisfy her.

"Maybe they just like her for herself," I said. "Maybe they're all just good friends."

"Well, they're certainly having a good time," Mom said, her eyes resting on the neighbors again. I wondered vaguely why she was paying so much attention to them. She usually made a point of ignoring other vacationers, unless they had connections with her own set. But now she smiled wistfully at them. "It's nice seeing people enjoy themselves so much, isn't it?" she asked.

10

The neighbors had arranged lawn chairs in a row facing the bay. They seemed fascinated by the sky and the water, pointing and gesturing, talking animatedly, sipping their drinks, frequently laughing. Their skin had a purplish cast in the fading light. I began to wonder, as their shapes grew indistinct, why they kept looking more and more often toward our house. Were they talking about us?

It was several hours later, Mom and Dad were watching television and I was rereading *The Puppet Masters*, when there was a knock on the front door.

"Maybe that's the people from next door," Mom said.

The cottage next door was the only other house on this stretch of road. "Who else?" Dad said, pushing himself out of his chair. I got up too, but he beat me to the door.

The woman from next door was wearing a sleeveless lavender cotton dress, and her hair was pinned up into a bun, exposing her long slender neck. Now, face to face, she seemed much taller than she had at a distance, several inches taller than me.

A smile hovered around the edges of her wide mouth, and in the dim porch light her eyes seemed as deep a shade of lavender as her dress. "Hello, I'm from nex. door and I'm sorry to bother you like this," she said. I couldn't place her accent. "I feel terribly *gênante*. It's just that we're trying to light a fire, and they don't seem to have provided us with any ... what's the word? Oh, yes, *tinder*. We were wondering if you might have any surplus, which we could burn just for tonight. We'll be sure to repay you in full tomorrow." She didn't meet our eyes as she spoke, but peered around us, as if she were trying to see as much as possible of the interior of our house.

"We have lots," Dad said. As he started for the fireplace

11

she stepped quickly into the house, almost bumping into me in her haste to get a good look at the living room.

"Good evening," Mom said, standing up and nodding pleasantly at the woman. "Barney, why don't you be a gentleman and carry the kindling over for her? Maybe they need some help settling in."

"Sure," I said, wondering what the matter was with Mom. Usually she would have been a little cold to a stranger barging in on us like this. Now she was actually sending me over to fraternize with the neighbors.

"Oh, thank you. And you wouldn't happen to have an extra one of those tide charts, by chance, would you?" the young woman asked, her gaze wandering toward the stairway.

"Yes, I'll get it," I said, forgetting to be shy.

She was looking at me now, and my eyes slid away from her. "That would be so gentle of you," she said warmly.

I got the tide chart, filled my arms with prickly kindling and pushed open the screen door. I waited while she remained inside for a long moment, then followed as she came striding out. In the darkness, the light from the cottage's picture window made a pale oblong on the sloping lawn. A crescent moon hung over the invisible black water.

"We're in fortune," the woman announced, holding open the screen door of the cottage as I stepped cautiously inside. Compared to the heavily curtained, overstuffed interior of the captain's house, the main room of the cottage seemed empty and bleak—bare white walls, gray linoleum floor, unmatching plastic furniture, with two metal floor lamps providing the harsh illumination. The men sat drinking wine at a wooden table in the center of the room.

The debris of a meal had been pushed aside, and some kind of a game seemed to be in progress. A board had been set up on the table, with movable pieces and colored cards and envelopes. A succulent, spicy smell lingered.

"That's a bonanza," said the man with the brown mustache, getting up to accept the kindling. I was aware, as he came toward me, of how large and powerfully built he was. "Thanks extremely," he said and lifted the big load of kindling from my arms as though it were a couple of match sticks.

"Hi," said the man with the blond beard, who was slenderer than the other, but wiry. "Did you get inside?" he asked the woman. Then he said "Oops!" and gulped down some wine.

Three pairs of lavender eyes watched me curiously now. And at that moment I noticed, in the corner by the fireplace, a pile of kindling. Why had they lied about it and borrowed more from us? Their strangeness intrigued me. "Anything you'd like to know about the area?" I asked, wanting an excuse to stay. "Or maybe I'm interrupting your game?"

"Of course you are, but please stay anyway," the woman said, smiling. "You're the only people around and we're wanting to find out about this quaint seacoast locale. Aren't we?"

"Yes, have some vino," said the blond man, reaching for the bottle.

"It's your tinder, stay and enjoy the fire," said the other man, kneeling at the hearth.

"This dump might actually be almost cozy when we get the fire going," the woman said, wrapping her dark arms around her shoulders. She stared at me "Sit down."

13

There was such authority and command in the way she spoke that I complied without thinking. What had happened to the petite, demure creature who had so coyly tried to cajole Ted to let them into our house? This person wouldn't have cajoled; she would have ordered. She seemed a different woman now, massive, brusque, in control.

We sat close together around the fireplace. I could tell that they really weren't too much older than me—they seemed about college age. The two men were shirtless, their taut bodies as deeply tanned as the woman's. I knew they had just arrived, but they looked as though they'd been living on the beach for months.

Zena, Manny, and Joe were their names. Before starting their game, they had gone for a moonlight swim, which was why Zena was so eager for a fire. "The water's superb at night," said Joe, the big man with the mustache. "It seems like a different element in the moonlight, phosphorescent and glittering and alive."

"I've never been swimming at night," I said. "I'd love to go sometime."

"You get a nice *frisson* because you can't see underwater," Zena said. "So you always have the notion that there might be something lurking there, observing you, waiting to pursue you if you try to get away. It's rather like our game."

"What I like is . . . you don't have to wear anything," said Manny, the blond man. He giggled.

"That's the natural and proper way to swim," Joe said.

"If only it didn't get so frigid at night," Zena said, shivering a little. "Though I never would have believed it this afternoon, when we were sitting in that filthy traffic jam. I felt like we were three eggs in *beurre noire*."

14

"Not butter! Rancid diesel oil would be more like it. Wonder what that would taste like."

"I didn't feel like a fried egg. I felt like *Tou-sha-pou*—you know, one of those Chinese steamed dumplings, those sickly sweet ones, filled with hot mashed prunes."

We were all laughing now. "Well, all I can say is, thank God we had our game to play," Zena said. "That was a truly capital round we had in that little car, stifling and *gemutlich* as it was."

"Capital, because you won," Manny pointed out.

"I like games too," I said. "Maybe we could play sometime."

I was impressed and a little awed by their easy, high-spirited banter. They could even have fun being stuck in a traffic jam. They seemed exotic, as though English was not their native language. And strangely enough, they really did seem interested in me. Maybe the second week of this vacation would be better than the first.

"This tide chart seems to be closely accurate, as far as you can tell?" Joe asked me.

"Yes," I said. "The tides are very extreme here, actually."

"Are they?" Joe asked me. "How so?"

"Well, at low tide, there's some areas where you can walk and walk and walk, and the water hardly ever gets past your waist."

"Do you know quite where?" They all seemed interested.

"Sure. I could show you. Tomorrow, maybe." I shrugged, and laughed self-consciously. "I don't have a real heavy schedule here."

"We could make it a charming little expedition," Zena said.

"Yes. Studying all the biota of this enchanting region," Manny said.

"Is this your first time in New England?" I asked them.

"Uh ... yes," Zena said.

"You must be from California then, right?" I went on. "Or Florida?" They didn't answer. "I mean ... you're so tanned."

"We travel a lot. We absorb the sun," Zena said.

"You don't have to work?" I asked.

"Curious fellow, isn't he," Joe said, putting a hand to his dark mustache.

"Our occupation gives us ample time to travel and explore," Zena explained, smiling. But there was a touch of impatience in her voice.

"Well, I'm pretty much of an expert on this whole coast," I said. "I could show you lots of things."

"That's pleasant," Joe said. "Barney? That's your name, right? Do there appear to be a lot of fishing boats in this immediate vicinity? Commercial or otherwise?"

"Sometimes they come around the island," I told him. "Ted has a cabin cruiser."

"How about excursion vessels, sightseers?"

"They don't come right around here." I was glad to be able to tell them so much. My familiarity with the area, limited as it was, might give them a reason for wanting to spend some time with me. "But there are several excursion boats out of Dunstable. Whale watches and dolphin watches and things. Would you like to go some day?"

"Love to," Manny said, with a funny little smile. "Joe adores dolphins. Don't you, Joe?"

"Yes. And octopi, too," Joe said.

Zena put her hand over her mouth and giggled like a little girl.

"They do any octopus fishing around here?" Joe went on, grinning at Manny now. "They do in some Greek settlements, I know. Remember Greece, Manny?"

"Oh, the way they bashed their poor little heads against the rocks, and left them out in the sun to dry!" Manny cried, rolling his eyes. "A sight I shall never forget!"

They were all laughing again. I didn't understand their secret joke, but I was amused by the way they were enjoying it. The enthusiasm with which they approached almost everything—especially their precious game—was appealing. They were younger and more playful than any adults I knew. And the amazing thing was, they continued to seem interested in me, and everything I had to say, asking lots of questions. They seemed fascinated by what I said about our house, absorbed and curiously motionless while I told them the story about the captain and his brother. I answered in detail their questions about the layout of the house and spent a lot of time describing the front bedroom, where I had been sleeping for the past week.

"Still, as nice as the view is, I wouldn't want to be locked up there for twenty years," I said.

They had turned out the floor lamps. In the shadowy, firelit room, Zena's eyes glittered like a cat's. "And the scratches Ted informed you about, were you able to discover them?" she asked, leaning toward me, her voice a gentle purr.

"Oh, sure. There's a lot of them, and some of them are deep, deeper than you'd think a person could make with his bare hands. He must have . . . spent a lot of time making them."

"And did they seem to fall into a kind of pattern or . . or tell a tale or anything?" Zena asked.

"No. They're completely senseless."

"I don't suppose there was anything else, uh ... unusual about the chamber, was there?" Zena said carefully. "Nothing odd, peculiar, that you or your parents might have stumbled on?"

It was a strange question, and I tried to make a joke out of it. "You mean like a dead body, or a ghost or something? Uh-uh. No such luck."

But they didn't seem to appreciate my wit. Barely moving their heads, their eyes met; three pairs of eyes meeting equally somehow, as though there were only two of them. And I thought of the jagged pits and troughs in the windowsills of my room, and I felt uneasy for the first time. A curtain flapped gently at the window. The others in the room remained as still as reptiles in the sun.

"So you travel a lot?" I said, breaking the uncomfortable silence. "That must be great. Where's your home base? What was your last trip?"

"You certainly do ask a plethora of questions," Manny said.

"I do?" I said. "Funny. It seems to me like *you're* the ones who've been asking *me* questions all evening."

"You know what?" Zena said abruptly. "All of a sudden I have a powerful nagging *itch* to get back to the game. How about it?"

"Nice," Manny said. "I *always* want to play the game."

They turned on the lights, pulled their chairs up to the table and sat down around the board I had noticed when I first came in. They hadn't asked me to play, so I stood behind Zena and looked down at it. It was the first chance I had had to study it, and I saw now that it was not like any board game I had ever encountered before.

"Hey, what game is this, anyway?" I asked, beginning

to feel extremely excited. It seemed to be a space fantasy, with dreamlike, but detailed, planets. "I love games, but I've never seen anything like this. Where on earth did you get it?"

There was a moment of silence. Then Zena said, "It's a very new game. I suppose it isn't even on the market yet. It's still being . . . uh, what's the word? . . . *Consumer tested*, that's it."

"How did you get your hands on it then?"

"Because . . ."

"Because we . . . encountered somebody in the business," Joe explained. "He borrowed us an advance set."

"It was the best event that ever happened to us," Manny said with conviction.

"It's a noble game," Joe said. "We've been playing it every night, and we still can't wrench ourselves away from it."

"But what's it called?" I asked again. "How do you play it?" I reached down to pick up one of the pieces.

"Don't touch, you'll distress it!" Zena slapped my hand a lot harder than seemed necessary.

"Questions, questions, questions," Joe murmured.

"But can't you just tell me the *name* of it?" I said, feeling a bit wounded.

"It's called Interstellar Pig," Zena said tartly. "We'd ask you to play, but we're in the middle of a three-person game. Perhaps another time."

Time! I had forgotten about it completely. How long had I been here? If I outstayed my welcome they might think I was a pest, and wouldn't take me along on any expeditions. "Well, it's probably time for me to go," I said. "But I would love to play it sometime."

"Uh-huh," Zena murmured, staring down at the board.

19

She moved her piece. "Hyperspace tunnel!" she announced triumphantly. "I'm going straight to Vavoosh."

They seemed to have forgotten I was there.

Mom and Dad were extremely curious about the neighbors, and dissatisfied by what I had to tell them. I'd been there for several hours, and yet I'd found out almost nothing about them. Mom and Dad quizzed me about their ages, their professions, their financial status, their relationships with one another, and where they came from. All I knew were their first names, that they traveled a lot and were addicted to Interstellar Pig.

"I'm surprised at you, Barney," Mom said. "You're usually so inquisitive."

And I was surprised at Mom and Dad. The neighbors were much younger than they were and had no obvious social position. Yet, for some reason, they were fascinated by them. It wasn't like them at all.

I looked carefully at the marks around the windows in my room that night. There was no message of any sort, only random wounds etched into the wood. When I got into bed, the scars, by some trick of the lamplight, emerged in sharp relief, like welts. I couldn't concentrate on my book, and turned out the light. The wheezing and gasping of the bedsprings as I tried to find a comfortable position made me think of an old man struggling to breathe. I assured myself that, ancient though it was, this could not possibly be the bed in which the prisoner had slept.

And if his ghost remained, it was too feeble a specter even to materialize in my dreams. It was Zena I dreamed of, leading me by the hand across the floor of a gigantic arena. It was patterned, like their game, with the images of planets and stars, and curving pathways of light. Zena was telling me over and over again something I could not grasp, something terribly important, of great beauty and significance.

3

The next day, Sunday, was what Mom calls a perfect day: blistering hot without a trace of cloud in the sky. Immediately after breakfast, she and Dad headed for the beach. It was the first such day we'd had for a while, and Mom was way behind on her tan. I accompanied them just to see who was there. It was well before noon, but the usual beach denizens were already ensconced: the old ladies with short-legged beach chairs and decks of cards, withered pink flesh drooping out of their ruffled suits; the shrieking toddlers with buckets and plastic swim toys; the gleaming adolescents, as stiff and carefully positioned as dark sarcophagi beside their radios, coming to life only to anoint themselves with more oil and solemnly, ritualistically press their blackened forearms together. In minutes, Mom had joined their ranks, her comparative pallor giv-

22

ing her the look of a greased corpse. I retreated to the safe darkness of the house.

I decided to take my book out to the front porch, which offered a view of the bay—not to mention a view of the patio next door, where our neighbors were setting up a table for breakfast. I didn't know them well enough yet to feel comfortable about joining them uninvited. But I did want them to see that I was available and idle, ready to be included in any games or expeditions. I pretended to read.

They still seemed preoccupied by their game of the night before. They spoke in hushed voices, but I could hear enough to tell that they were arguing about the best escape route from a maze on some foreign planet.

Then, abruptly, and in a much louder voice, Zena announced, "These tomatoes taste ersatz."

Joe remarked in equally artificial tones that the word *ersatz* came from a German noun meaning "substitute," first used in 1875. I wondered if they had realized I was listening, and were changing the subject for my benefit.

"How come I never know obscure little data like that?" asked Manny.

"Because you never read a word besides fantasy and science fiction," said Zena disdainfully.

"You should mention! Regard the books you brought here. *The Flame, the Power and the Passion; The Body in the Library.*"

"But I also brought *Principles of Intensive Psychotherapy,*" she pointed out. "Unlike you, I'm not totally self-involved."

They were both beginning to giggle. "Self-involved!" Manny exclaimed. "How can anybody vain enough to let her fingernails grow as grotesquely long as yours talk

23

about self-involved? Observe her, Joe. She can barely even grasp her coffee cup with those claws."

"Vain!" she exploded. "You don't think it's vain to obsess about how evenly your beard is trimmed, not to mention bleach it! And don't try to deny it. I glimpsed that bottle of peroxide in your drawer."

"You prying bitch!" Manny cried. Zena threw back her head and laughed.

"Cut it out, you two," said Joe. "Look at the island. See how much clearer it is in the morning light. It looks nearly twice as close as it did yesterday afternoon."

"I wonder if we could swim out to it," Zena said. "Not you, Manny, of course. We all know you'd never make it. But Joe and I might be—"

"It's too distant to swim," Joe interrupted, before they had a chance to get started again. "Windsurfing's the means. One of these days we should borrow some boards and sail on over there."

"Grand idea!"

I listened, not turning any pages. Yet somehow they managed to startle me a moment later by appearing without any warning at the bottom of the porch steps. Why hadn't I noticed them getting up and coming over?

The men wore only running shorts and sandals; Zena had on the brief denim cutoffs and halter top. "Good morning, Barney," she said in her deep voice, smiling. "We just wandered over to see if everything was serene." Her legs looked wonderful.

"After we kept you up late and fed you intoxicating beverages and everything," Manny put in.

"I'm fine," I mumbled. Their unexpected arrival had brought back all my original shyness.

24

"You just seemed so bereft and deserted, all by yourself here," said Zena, moving smoothly up the steps. "Your parents abandoned you for the beach, huh?"

"Yes, we were kind of surprised to see *anyone* at home on a day like this," Manny said.

Zena shot him a glance and Joe looked away. It occurred to me, though I knew it was ridiculous, that they had been hoping we would all be at the beach today. But why should that make any difference to them?

Zena sat down on the porch railing across from my chair, watching me with that slight smile, one hand on a brown thigh. The men stood less comfortably at the top of the steps. They seemed to be expecting me to do something. "I can't lie out in the sun," I said "I always burn."

"It's because you're a redhead," said Joe, with a hollow little click of the teeth.

"Seems like an inappropriate place for your family to come for a vacation, in that case," Zena said sympathetically. "Not thoughtful to you."

"Mom has friends who come here. And I have a lot to read," I said, feeling pitiful—what would they think of someone who spent his vacation *reading*? I felt a blush coming on.

"What are you reading?" Manny inquired. I held the book in front of my face. "Oh, I *love* science fiction," he said, clasping his hands together fervently. "But I haven't read that volume. What's it about?"

"It's about these aliens that invade the earth," I said. "These sort of sluglike things, like exposed brains, that attach themselves to people's backs and control them."

"How loathsome," Zena said, and turned down the corners of her mouth.

25

"Not to mention biologically naive," Joe said, chuckling. "There's no way an organism like that could evolve naturally."

"Why not?" I said, wanting to defend my taste in literature. "Nobody knows what conditions might be like on other planets. Anything could be possible, couldn't it?"

Joe stroked his mustache.

"Well I think it sounds enchanting," Manny said. "I love creepy stories like that. It reminds me of our game. Can I borrow the book when you're through?"

"Sure," I said. "Hey, would you guys like to go on one of those excursion—"

"Speaking of creepy stories," Zena firmly interrupted me. "We were all entertained by the story you told us last night, about this house. You made us rather intrigued. Would you disapprove if we had a peek inside, just so we could see where it really happened?"

"I guess not," I said. Something about her request didn't ring true. It wasn't what *I* had said that had kindled their interest—they had wanted to look inside the house yesterday, the moment they had arrived, before I had told them the story about it. I remembered what Ted had said about their reaction when they couldn't rent the house themselves. As I held the door open for them, I had the peculiar sensation that I was making a mistake. But I dismissed it immediately. I wanted to play the authority and show them around.

"Gee, it's so much more *confortable* than our place," Manny said, his eyes wandering over the wood paneling. "As though the person who built it actually planned to reside here."

"But it's so dark," Zena said. She looked out the dining

26

room windows. "And you can't even see the water. Our monstrosity next door gets in the way."

"He was right when he said the cottage had a better view," Joe said, peering inside the fireplace.

"Look at this!" Manny called from the kitchen. "You could actually *cook* in here."

The rest of us trooped in after him. "Do you three have some kind of special interest in old houses?" I asked.

"Sure, Barney," Zena said, peering into the cabinet under the sink. Joe was opening and shutting the cupboards and Manny was poking around in the refrigerator.

"This thing is twice as great as ours," he said. "Can you believe this? Frozen scrambled egg substitute. *Margarine!*" He sounded shocked.

"Dad has to watch his cholesterol," I explained. "Hey, listen, there's some really famous old houses over in Dunstable. Kind of museums. Maybe we could go see them sometime."

"Sure, Barney," Zena said, exploring the broom closet.

Manny was going through the drawers of cooking utensils. "Look at all the tools that are included with this place. Much more than they provide for the cottage," he said.

Were they actually looking for something, or just making jealous comparisons between our house and theirs? I was beginning to find their behavior a little annoying. "You wanted this place, didn't you," I said bluntly.

"What do you mean?" Zena turned around and stared at me.

"That's what Ted said. You wanted this house, not the cottage."

27

"Well you have to admit, it *is* nicer," Manny explained reasonably.

"Yes, but since you hadn't seen it, how did you know? And what are you looking for now?"

"Perceptive, aren't you, Barney," Joe said. But it didn't sound like a compliment. "You're astute; we do have an interest in old houses. It's kind of a hobby, a *harmless* one. Like our game. You don't have any objection to our looking around, do you?"

"Uh . . . no, I guess not," I said, feeling foolish.

"Well, if you'd stop asking questions and let us get on with it, then perhaps we'd have time later to teach you our game. Just drop over after lunch. Sound fair enough?"

"Sure, that would be great."

"Agreed." He pulled open the basement door. "Where's the light?"

"On the left."

There wasn't much to see down there, just a few pieces of the usual basement junk and a lot of pipes. But the three of them behaved as though they had discovered an Egyptian crypt that had been sealed up for the last five thousand years. They ran around exclaiming and poking through the moldy debris. Did they really expect to find something valuable?

Watching them made me feel a little edgy, but I didn't have the nerve to ask them to stop, so I went back upstairs and waited in the living room. I began to wonder what would happen if Mom and Dad returned and found them in the house. It had been well over an hour since I had left the beach.

Our three neighbors almost didn't notice me on their way through the living room to the stairway to the second floor. Only after I coughed did Manny say, "Oh, is it agreeable if we go upstairs?" but he didn't even slow down.

Then Zena turned back from the landing, abruptly, as though she had just remembered something, and said, "Would you like to show us your room, Barney?"

I trotted after them, remembering that the bed wasn't made and hoping I hadn't left any dirty underwear lying around. I needn't have worried, though. They did Mom and Dad's room before mine. Most people will just stand politely in the doorway to a bedroom and peer inside, but not these three. They made a thorough search, poking into the closet and under the bed, examining the windows, opening the dresser drawers. It didn't make sense; *my* room was the one with historical interest. Still, it gave me a chance to dash ahead of them and clean up.

When they finally did reach my room, they didn't bother making even a token attempt to pay attention to me. It was I who waited politely in the doorway, sensing that it was important to keep out of their way. The banter stopped. Their faces hardened and withdrew. More like archeologists than ever, they examined the paneling and the windows in minutest detail, unblinking, their fingers stroking the wood with the reverent intensity of the blind. In the silence I became aware of the surf and the bird cries, and listened to the static bleat of a radio rise and fall in volume as some kids carried it partway up the road and then turned back.

I felt shut out and restless, but I was afraid to make a sound. I began to wonder how I was ever going to get rid of them. Almost two hours now had gone by since I had left Mom and Dad at the beach. I knew they weren't going to let themselves burn, and it was also lunchtime. Surreptitiously, I crept into the room and looked over their shoulders out the window.

The view from upstairs was not obstructed by the one-story cottage next door. The ocean air was so clear that, even though Mom and Dad were about a hundred yards away, I could easily read Mom's expression as they passed the kids with the radio—she wondered why they were coming down *our* dead-end road. And she probably wouldn't like it if she knew how thoroughly the people from next door had gone through our belongings. She might think they were casing the place to see if there was anything to steal, and maybe she would be right. What else could they be doing? And if they did end up stealing anything, it would be my fault.

There was no time to stand around berating myself. Even if the neighbors were perfectly innocent, I still didn't want Mom to find them in the house.

But they hadn't even noticed Mom and Dad; they were behaving like zombies.

"Uh, listen . . . uh, those are my parents coming back," I faltered, twisting my hands. "See?"

They started, like people coming out of a trance, and froze for a moment. Then they turned slowly to look at me, their faces still dead.

"They might not understand what you're doing in our house," I went on. "I think, maybe you should go now."

It was as though they did not know who or what I was, as though they really *couldn't* see or even hear me. Their icy unresponsive stares cut me off like a solid wall; I had never felt so supremely unnecessary. But *they* were the ones who were acting like crazy people, not me. What was the matter with them? Wasn't there anything I could say to get them to respond?

"I'm not kidding," I said. "It could be embarrassing. And . . . and then I might not be able to ask you back to see this house again."

Then they woke up, like a freeze-frame melting back into action. Joe shook his head irritably and glanced out the window; Manny ran a hand through his hair. Zena frowned and moved toward me. "Don't worry, Barney," she said, "we won't get you in any trouble."

Suddenly they were moving fast. Before I knew it I was running after them into the kitchen. "Thanks for the tour, Barney," Zena said. "And I think you're accurate about your parents. It might be well if they didn't know we'd been here."

"Can I come over, after lunch like you said?" I asked, before agreeing to keep their visit a secret.

"Sure, sure, Barney. Come on over. We'll do something fun, perhaps play a round of the game," Zena said, pulling open the back door.

"Yes, come for a visit," Manny echoed as though he meant it, and they were gone.

They managed to get across the yard and back to their cottage without Mom and Dad noticing a thing. It was a small thing, their ability to get around without attracting attention, but it had the adeptness of a skill acquired with practice. It was the same as the way they had so thoroughly searched the house, working efficiently—another acquired skill. As I went over it in my mind, I began to realize that they really hadn't missed a single cupboard or closet.

Yet it was hard to believe that they were thieves. If that

was the case, they were too good to waste their time at a dump like this, where there was obviously nothing of much value and only one family to steal from. Thieves with their apparent expertise would be working large and expensive resorts, where the booty would be worth something.

But if they weren't thieves, then what were they?

From the dining room window I watched the neighbors greet Mom and Dad from their front patio, where they were already relaxing by the time Mom and Dad reached it. They spoke pleasantly together, until the neighbors got up and went inside.

"... so impressive, that deep sense of commitment, don't you think?" Mom was saying, as they came into the house. "But they're such cheerful young men, not at all stuffy. I'll bet they're doctors. That's why they give that impression of social responsibility."

"Not just the men," Dad said. "The girl seemed so *involved* in the problem of poverty, so deeply concerned. But charming at the same time. I'll bet she's a doctor too."

"Probably a social worker—she doesn't seem as bright as the men."

I was amazed. Mom and Dad weren't stupid, yet their impression of the neighbors was totally out of whack. Responsibility? Concern with poverty? I wanted to scream with laughter. But I kept quiet.

I would take advantage of the neighbors' invitation and visit them this afternoon. But this time I would turn the tables; this time *I* would be the one to find out about *them*.

But when I went over an hour or so later there was no answer to my knock. The house was empty, and unlocked. For a moment I felt hurt that they had forgotten their invitation and gone off without me. Then I saw I was being silly; they had provided me with exactly the opportunity I wanted. I felt a prickling of excitement—I hadn't expected the situation to be reversed quite this neatly. It was like some funny game of taking turns, and I barely hesitated on the threshold.

And now I wonder: How differently would things have ended if I hadn't found what I did that day?

4

In the bright sunlight, their cheap little cottage was about as sinister as a dairy bar, which was actually what it looked like from the outside. The inside, with its linoleums and plastic furniture and picture windows, was equally eerie. If the place really had been dark and mysterious, I probably wouldn't have had the nerve to sneak inside at all. As it was, the fact that I was secretly entering someone else's place to try to search out information about them was exciting enough. And I didn't even have to feel guilty. They were the ones who had started it, after all; they were only getting what they deserved.

There was not much to poke into in the barren living room. A chartreuse plastic easy chair squatted on one side of the fireplace, a maroon one on the other side, and facing it, a pink painted wicker love seat, beginning to unravel. The square wooden dining table with captain's chairs around it was placed beside the largest window overlooking the water. The board game was no longer on the table, or anywhere else to be found. I was disappointed. I had been looking forward to examining it.

I leafed quickly through the books and periodicals on the mantel and tabletop—collections of horror stories, the Sunday *New York Times, People* magazine, some lurid mysteries, a large illustrated paperback about windsurfing. Nothing to learn there.

The kitchen was smaller and more primitive than ours, the haphazard collection of plates and cups arranged on open pine shelving, the meager assortment of pots and pans under the sink. I didn't go through it very thoroughly. Who ever kept anything important in the kitchen? If anything was to be found, it would have to be in one of the bedrooms. I pushed open the flimsy door to the bedroom beside the kitchen.

In the darkness, a deformed face swam toward me, all huge bulbous forehead, with tiny squashed-together eyes and two pursed, fishlike mouths hanging from the nonexistent chin.

I hardly shrieked much at all, and quickly complimented myself on how cool I was to realize, without even bolting from the house, that it was merely a warped mirror on the opposite wall. But I turned on the light immediately. There was a sagging double bed, a narrow closet, and a small dresser. And nothing to be found but men's clothes and a very large assortment of toiletries.

Each of them had a separate bedroom, I learned that much. I came to Zena's last. The lingerie, much of it with delicate lacy embroidery, I found particularly interesting. It smelled like Zena's perfume. And if I hadn't taken the time to go through it carefully, I never would have found the photocopied sheets paper-clipped together, pushed off into the bottom corner of the drawer.

And if Zena hadn't underlined certain passages in red ink, and scribbled flamboyant comments in the margins, I probably wouldn't even have given the papers a second glance. But the marks made me curious, and I sank down on her bed and began to read.

On my way over to their house, I hadn't thought much about their car being there, since I had assumed they were at home. And when I saw that they weren't home, I forgot to think about the car at all. If I *had* thought about it, I might not have stretched out so comfortably in her room and forgotten where I was; I might have been better prepared to expect them to return suddenly and without warning.

The papers were a photocopy of an old diary, scratched in archaic longhand, smudged and stained and difficult to read. But I persisted: The heavy underlining meant that Zena had thought the document was extremely important.

20 September 1864

Last night, only two minutes past two bells it was, an unpredicted, unexplained comet sighted, streaking so slowly across the breadth of the night sky that all men on watch were able clearly to see it, creating much uproar and hullabaloo, and cries of "Money, money, money!" I like it not. Long have I studied the skies, and yet have never seen celestial body move in such an erratic course.

21 September 1864

It is with the utmost reluctance that I put pen to paper on this most grievous day, when for shame alone my soul would long rather to *expunge* from this account, than record for all posterity, these most black and bitter events.

Only yesterday it was, at six bells, that the survivor was sighted from the crow's nest; yet now it seems many months, rather than mere fleeting hours, ago, that the tragedy commenced. The body, clinging to the blackened spars, was seen to appear to move; I could not but order a lifeboat to the rescue. And, indeed, when he was borne to the deck, I was able to ascertain that the foreign mariner *did* breathe, and ordered brandy and poultices, and did all in my limited power to soothe and refresh the invalid; and only minutes later was rewarded by the opening of his bloodshot eyes, and by his garbled and unintelligible expressions of gratitude. Though his tongue was as outlandish as his garb, I perceived nevertheless a miraculous *calm* in the face of such dire circumstances.

By this time, of course, I had realized what this document was. This was even better than the article Ted had mentioned. Zena had managed to dig up Captain Latham's own handwritten account of the tragedy, probably from his log, and had made photocopies of it. Their behavior in our house this morning now began to make a little more sense. Clearly, they had some intense personal interest in the morbid little incident.

But what was their interest? And why had they pretended to know nothing about the story last night? They knew more than I did—they had brought these papers with them. The sheets were creased and smudged and torn in places, as though they had been studied for weeks. It seemed now that they had come here precisely *because* of the captain's story, despite the fact that they claimed they had never heard it before. Why did they have to be so secretive?

Sunlight poured through the window onto the fragrant unmade bed. I felt a slight chill. This was not the time to speculate about their motivation, I told myself. So they had some reason to be secretive. In that case, I had better finish reading now, while I had the chance.

And if, perhaps, the poor soul had been less debilitated by the ravages of thirst and extreme fatigue, then perhaps some form of meaningful intercourse could have been established, so that, as we are as widely ranging a group of seamen as is to be found on any ship that sails the seas, there might have been one among us who could have been enabled to deduce the *origin* of our unfortunate new companion. Yet it was not to be, for quickly he relapsed again into his somnolent state; and, though our ministrations had appeared to offer him some refreshment, as evidenced by the improved tone of his complexion, which, on his being brought aboard, had displayed a morbid greenish pallor underneath the pitiless fiery blandishments of the sun but was now of a more sanguine, almost lavender hue, his physical condition was as yet too dangerously *tenuous* to allow us to attempt to question him further; and, instead, I had him borne with utmost care to my own cabin; and there I had him installed with Ethan, my beloved, trusted, gentle Ethan, to tend to him, with his special loving simplicity, as I went about my already sorely interrupted duties.

When I returned, my brother Ethan knelt upon the floor in an attitude of prayer. The shape on my bed was covered completely by bedclothes, and my first thought was that the foreigner had died of natural causes, and that my brother was praying for his soul. I was roused at once to anger. "And did I not instruct you to send word at once of any change in his condition?" I cried. But my brother

38

remained crouched, his face hidden from me, a strange trinket clenched in his hand. "Why did you not heed me?" I demanded. "With my knowledge, I might have prolonged his life!" Still, my brother did not move or speak, adding more fire to my fury. "Speak, man! You are not deaf and dumb!" I bellowed, and shook him violently by his collar.

And then my brother slowly turned to gaze upon me, and I perceived that he had not been praying but rather weeping like a babe. Yet, it was not sorrow that transformed his eyes, but *horror*, horror of such depth that it was as though he looked not upon my countenance, but upon the countenance of some fiend of the pit.

His first feeble utterance was, "It is the Devil, the Devil, he revealed his true nature to me, Tobias. I had to do it. It is the Devil."

Again, weeping overcame him. I pushed him aside with an oath and tore the bedclothes from the shape beneath. And there I—

"But Manny, I'm about ten shades darker than you. Just look!" Zena cried from the front of the house. There was a burst of laughter, and footsteps on the small cement patio.

If they had been driving, and I had heard the car approach, I would have had plenty of time to put things in order, and maybe even get out the back. As it was, I had no chance to open the correct drawer, rearrange its contents, and replace the document as I had found it. I didn't think much; I just shoved the papers into my back pocket and leapt off the bed and out of the room. It was bad enough to be discovered inside their house at all, but to be found snooping around in Zena's bedroom would be unthinkable. I would have to try to replace the document later.

When they marched through the front door seconds later, I was standing with my arm flung across the mantel, like someone in an old-fashioned play, pretending to look at a book.

"Barney! What are you doing here?"

What I was doing was blushing furiously. I couldn't tell whether they were angry or merely surprised. "Well, uh, you asked me to come over, but nobody was here, so I thought . . . you wouldn't mind if I just read this book for a minute."

They looked at one another slowly; then Zena was giggling. She had a rapid, high-pitched, silly giggle, like a teenager's, that bore no relation to her husky speaking voice. "And just what is it that you found to read, Barney, hmmmmm?" she asked teasingly, moving toward me and lifting her eyebrows.

She didn't seem to be angry, but I wondered how she would feel if she knew what I really had been reading. I looked at the book in my hand for the first time. "When the aversive stimulus is the withdrawal of positive reinforcement," said the paragraph at the top of the page, "the resulting nonreinforcement of enough items . . ."

"I see, *A Psychological Approach to Abnormal Behavior*," Zena said, reading the title on the jacket. "A little weighty for a Sunday afternoon, but certainly a step up from science fiction. So you're an abnormal psychology enthusiast, is that it?"

"I . . . well I just . . . it seemed . . ."

"Well who *isn't* interested in abnormal psychology?" Manny demanded, hurrying over to the fireplace to de-

40

fend me. "I love looking in volumes like that and discovering how abnormal *I* am."

"You have to look in a *book*?" Zena asked him.

"Everybody's abnormal, when you come to the bottom of it," said Joe, glancing at his watch. "Who's coming with me—to pick up the windsurfers?"

"I'll go," Manny said.

"I think I'll stay here and entertain Barney," Zena said. "Also, I need to do some work on my tan."

"Hey, that's not fair," Manny whined, quickly holding his arm up to hers and comparing them with a critical eye.

"Relax, Manny, we'll take the top down," Joe said. "Everybody knows you tan better in a moving vehicle than when you're just lying still."

"Is that really true?"

"Well *I* never heard of it before," Zena said.

"It's because of relativity and time dilation," Joe explained with a straight face. "The greater your velocity, the slower time moves for you, so you have more time in the sun. Also, you age slower, so you stay younger looking."

"No, but wait a moment," Manny said, sounding really concerned. "If time slows down for you, then it actually signifies you have *less* time in the sun than—"

"If you don't get going now, it'll be too late to get *any* sun, even if you travel at the speed of light," Zena said impatiently.

"Come on, Manny."

And then, in that strange sudden way, the two men were gone. "Well, perhaps now we can get to discover each other, Barney," Zena said, her smile widening. "Perhaps we could even play the game."

41

5

She made a pitcher of lemonade and cajoled me relentlessly to sit with her out on the patio in the sun, insisting that it was too late in the day to get a bad burn, and offering me a tube of protective cream. I continued to balk. Finally she said, "Do you want a private lesson in Interstellar Pig or not?"

"Sure I do!" I was flattered, and hoped I'd be a worthy opponent.

"All right, I'll teach you a lesson, but I refuse to stay inside. We do it outside or not at all."

"But ..."

"This is your final chance, Barney. And if you don't take it, I warn you, the others won't want to play with you."

"Oh, all right."

42

She handed me the lemonade pitcher and two glasses, and draped towels over my arm. "Take this outside, and take your shirt off and slather that cream all over you. I'll get the board."

She didn't want me to know where they kept the board, it seemed. What if it was in the drawer where the document had been, and she noticed it was missing? I felt a sudden burst of panic. But the board hadn't been in that drawer, I assured myself, spreading out the towels—if it had been, I would have seen it.

"Obey me, Barney, off with the shirt and on with the cream," she said, coming out with the board. She had changed into her bikini.

Obediently, I took off my shirt and applied the cream. My body was so white, compared to hers, that we could have been members of different species.

She set down the board and then sank to her knees on the towel and tossed back her hair. Muscles rippled on her abdomen. She opened the board between the two towels.

I shaded my eyes with my hands and peered down at it. The background was black, sprinkled with stars. The stars seemed to be tiny reflectors, for they glowed—unblinking—as they would in space. They also varied in intensity, from big bright ones to pale clusters, distant nebulae so vague they were difficult to see in the bright sunlight, in shapes of spirals and crabs and amorphous clouds.

The effect was so realistic that it could have been a vast photograph of the cosmos, taken by an outer space probe—if it hadn't been for the planets. They were strewn across the void, appearing to float above the board in startling three-dimensional relief. There was a fat bulbous one aswirl in luminous gasses. Several sported dazzling complex colored rings that made Saturn's look as dull as Hula Hoops. There were planets of deserts and terrifying jagged mountains; lonely barren pockmarked planets as dead as the moon.

"Comprehend?" Zena was saying. "The objective is to have The Piggy in your hand when the alarm goes off at the end. You will stop at *nothing* to gain possession of it. Otherwise, when the alarm goes, you and your home planet will be destroyed. Grasp it? Now, there are lots of manners of getting hold of The Piggy and preserving it from the other players. For instance, you can ..."

I wasn't really listening, hypnotized by the board. The larger stars seemed to be arranged in a kind of pattern— like the warped reflection of a chessboard grid in a distorting mirror—that undulated across the entire board. As if the stars could be used as a kind of path of stepping stones. And there were also several absolutely empty spots, small starless areas carefully contoured to give the impression that they were funnels, leading down into nothingness. Black holes?

"... so that if you happen to be a water-breathing gill man from Thrilb, you can't set foot on Vavoosh without special breathing equipment, or you'll drown in boiling ammonia—not a pretty way to go. Or let's suggest you're an arachnoid nymph from Vavoosh, and you somehow end up on Mbridlengile, God forbid. The carnivorous lichen on Mbridlengile"—she pronounced it with a soft *g*—"aren't terribly sapient, but they're thorough. It would take them quite a time to digest you, and you'd be conscious for most of it—they go for the brain last." She nodded eagerly at me. "Okay, Barney? Prepared to play?"

I had barely been listening to her and had no idea what

44

she was talking about. It seemed complicated and grisly. "It's kind of hard to take it all in so fast," I said. "Could you just go over it once more?"

She rolled her eyes. "You're going to have to be a little quicker on the uptake, Barney. This game goes *vite*. Maybe I miscalculated your abilities."

"I'm a whiz at games," I insisted. "I just got distracted by the board. You have to admit it's pretty spectacular. Please, this time I'll pay attention."

She sighed. "Well see that you do. Now. There are three kinds of cards: character cards, attribute cards, and instruction cards," she said, expertly shuffling one of the packs. "First you deal the character cards." She began laying cards out, upside down, on the cement beside the board. They were black on the back.

"Those are the character cards?" I asked her.

"Uh-huh," she said, her tongue between her teeth.

"But we don't get to see them? We don't get to choose which character we want to be?"

"Decidedly not. It's random, like life. Whatever creature you turn out to be determines what kind of atmosphere and temperature you need to stay alive—your strengths and weaknesses."

"But where do you get that information?"

"From the rule book." She patted a fat volume on the towel beside her. "Go ahead, Barney. Pick."

I hesitated. It seemed that a lot depended on the character you turned out to be. It was an unusual experience for me to be sitting out on the hilltop in the warm sun above the brightly crinkling, endless bay. But I wasn't noticing any of it.

"You go first," I said.

"The dealer doesn't pick first. Come, Barney. Take one," she urged me.

I picked the card that would be my character and held it up to my eyes, carefully shielding it from Zena. Drawn in lifelike detail on the card was a bubbling, gluey mass, a thick puddle of pink slime. Underneath it, enclosed in a circle, was a drawing of what seemed to be a single cell— apparently one of the individual units that made up the mass. The cell looked like a squashed wad of bubble gum, with faintly bluish nerves branching through it.

"Ugh!" I couldn't help saying, as I pressed the card against my chest. *This* was the character I was supposed to be?

Zena was studying her card with a little smile. She glanced at me and giggled. "No necessity to secrete it, Barney. We all have to know what characters the other players are." She flipped her card over, displaying a fat, spiderlike creature with eight jointed legs. Its face might have resembled a human female's, except that the top half of the head was immensely swollen, to make room for huge faceted eyes. "I'm Zulma, an arachnoid nymph from Vavoosh," she introduced herself. "I'm not terribly agile in all environments, but I *am* quite brilliant, and marvelously sneaky. Who are you?"

"This yucky thing," I said, showing her. "Couldn't I pick another one?"

"The carnivorous lichen from Mbridlengile!" she cried. "They're fabulous!"

I studied the card again, doubtfully. "I can't exactly see myself *identifying* with it. Couldn't I pick another?"

"Against the rules," she said flatly. "You're going to have to stop being so prejudiced and provincial. How do you think *you* look to *them*? You don't appreciate how fortunate you are. Didn't you hear what I said about the lichen previously, Barney? They can eat anything—no creature is safe from them. And they're incredibly tough. They can survive at any temperature and in any atmosphere *without* cumbersome equipment like breathing gear—remember that, Barney—as long as there is something for them to dine upon. To the lichen, to eat *is* to breathe. Of course, they are rather less sapient than most other gaming species—my character, Zulma, the arachnoid nymph, is about one hundred times as intelligent as they are—but they do make up for it to some amount by—"

"But how do you know all that?" I said.

"I told you. It's in the rule book." She handed me the volume.

I looked up my character. For a moment—possibly because of the glare of the sun—the lines of print shimmered illegibly. But quickly my eyes adjusted.

Kingdom: Fungi

Phylum: Mollusca

Order: Holotricha

Genus & Species: Lichenes thallophytis

Common Name: Lichen

Personal Name: Not applicable

Sex: Not applicable

Intelligence: IRSC 150

Habitat: Surface of the planet
Mbridlengile

Diet: The lichen can obtain adequate sustenance from all known plants and animals. The lichen do, however, seem to exhibit a preference for the neural tissue of more intelligent animal species, taking especial relish in devouring living, conscious, functioning brain matter.

General Remarks: Like certain primitive marine invertebrates, the lichen bridge the narrow gap between plant and animal. They live in colonies of hundreds or thousands of individual cells. Though the cells themselves do not possess senses as they are known to higher animal species, each cell is capable of absorbing chemical data from its immediate surface and transmitting it to the rest of the colony. In this way, the colony *as a whole* can be said to "see" its environment, even in the absence of light. The individual cells are incapable of passing on false information; they cannot "lie" to one another—such behavior would have no survival value for the colony. The colonies are ambulatory, and though their pace is necessarily slower than that of most animals, they are capable of eating through almost any obstacle to their progress.

"You don't have to *memorize* it, Barney. You can check the details whenever you want."

I looked up. Sunlight hammered onto the cement patio, which sent up sheets of heat that caused Zena's hands, shuffling another pile of cards, to waver before my eyes. Sweat trickled down my ribs, washing away the cream, but I hardly felt it. There is no heat in interstellar space.

"Your deal," she said, handing me the cards.

"Which cards are these?"

"Attribute cards—things like special powers and equipment—and one of them is The Piggy. Obviously, most characters need equipment that allows them to breathe in other atmospheres, so they can get to other planets. Even the lichen sometimes need weapons, and vehicles, and protection."

"That makes it complicated," I said.

"Challenging is the word, Barney. You'll get the droop of it. Now are you going to deal or not? And these cards are kept secret, by the way."

I began to deal them slowly, upside down. "Why is the important card called The Piggy?"

"I don't know. That's just what they've always called it."

"What does The Piggy do?"

"Nothing. It exhibits no power at all, during the course of the game. But it is *the* single most vital card. If you don't have The Piggy when the alarm goes off, you and your home planet are destroyed. The only survivor is the one who holds The Piggy at the end of the game. Okay?"

"I guess so," I said, although destroying all the players but one—not to mention their planets—seemed a little extreme.

I finished dealing. Zena gathered up her cards and studied them, chewing on her lip. "Oh, yes, you can only hold six cards in your hand at one time," she told me. "The rest of them have to be secreted away, on various planets. There's an envelope for each planet on the board. It's a wise advantage to stash your cards on planets that are less poisonous to you. Or if you have certain special equipment, you may want to secrete it on a planet where the equipment will be of use."

"But—"

"I'm almost concluded. You'll snatch on when we start to play. The most important thing is to find a good hiding place for The Piggy. You want it to be impossible for the others to find, but easy for you to travel to by the end of the game."

"But why not just keep it in your hand all the time, so that you'll be sure to have it at the end?"

"It's not secure enough in your hand. You may be in direct combat with someone and have to sacrifice a card. The optimum place for The Piggy is on some planet that's lethal to everyone else, but comfortable for you. And it's also a wise idea to surround it with various traps, or powerful guardians, so even if an opponent discovers it, he'll die before he can get it."

The attribute cards included many types of breathing apparatus. There were also ray guns and bombs and missiles. There were even primitive things like ropes and flashlights and dehydrated food. And there were some things I didn't understand, like Portable Instant Impermeable Time-Released Cryogenic Vault, or Portable Access to the Fifth-Dimensional Matrix. No card in my hand said anything about a Piggy. Since there were only two of us, that meant Zena had it. So I had to get it away from her.

I decided not to be intimidated. The game was so complicated, and involved so much information, that there was no hope of my planning an intelligent strategy this time. The only way to learn was to plunge in and play by pure instinct, not worrying about winning or losing. She had said this was a lesson, not a real game anyway.

She laid out the planetary envelopes in two neat lines.

Each was printed with a duplicate of one of the planets from the board and its name. We rolled dice to determine who picked first. I chose my planets without thinking too much about it, and distributed my cards among them. When we had both finished, Zena put all the filled envelopes into a black bag, reminding me that no envelopes could be opened until one's character had landed on the corresponding planet on the board. She placed a little black figure representing Zulma on Vavoosh, her home planet. She placed a pink one, representing the lichen, on Mbridlengile. Then she placed a small white disk, about an inch in diameter and half an inch thick, beside the bag of envelopes. "This is the timer," she said, one finger poised above a button on its edge. She stared at me. "Ready to go?"

"Wait," I said. "How long do we have before it goes off?"

"You'll be able to see. Now can we *please play*?"

"Go ahead."

She pressed the button. Zena won the first roll and moved first. "One two three four five six," she counted, moving her piece along the curving pathway of stars.

I rolled a 9, and moved nine stars in the direction of the planet Flaeioub. It was the planet Zena had picked first, and so I figured it was important to her, and that maybe she had hidden The Piggy there. But as I set the lichen down on the ninth star, the star began blinking on and off. "What does that mean?" I said, startled.

"You have to pull an instruction card. It's right there."

The edge of a white card was poking out of a slot in the middle of the board. "Is it random, or what?" I asked.

"Yes, Barney, it's random. It can happen on any star,"

Zena said, her voice sounding a little strained. "And will you speed up? Observe how much time is elapsed already!"

I glanced over at the timer. A small curved area of black had appeared at the right-hand edge of the disk.

"Oh, I get it," I said brightly. "The time's up when the whole thing goes black."

"Brilliant induction!" Zena snapped. "Pull out the card!"

I pulled it out. Once again, the sun's glare made the writing seem to squirm for an instant. Then I read, "Minor malfunction in communications system. Go into orbit around nearest foreign planet and sacrifice next two turns making repairs."

"That's Ja-Ja-Bee, right there," Zena said. "Go on, go into orbit."

"I have to miss my next two turns?"

"That's what it instructs." She smiled at me.

I orbited impatiently around Ja-Ja-Bee, which had a climate so frigid that glaciers covered the entire planet. At least the card had not instructed me to land there.

Zena, meanwhile, whistling happily, rolled a 9 and then a 12, moving ever closer to Flaeioub, the planet most important to her, because she had picked it first. Was she trying to get there ahead of me, to protect The Piggy? Or was she merely leading me on a wild-goose chase? I whiled away the time in orbit checking out the information about Flaeioub from the rule book. There was enough data there to keep me occupied for weeks. Flaeioub was inhabited by gas bags, flying octopi with claws who were kept aloft by their inflated heads. The atmosphere was high in hydrogen, which didn't matter to the lichen, but meant that Zulma would need breathing gear. Under the surface of the planet was an intricate maze of deep, lightless caverns, which would make it a good hiding place for The Piggy. Zulma would need special glasses in order to see in the caverns, but the lichen would be able to get around without equipment, since they could "see" without light, according to the rule book.

The planet Flaeioub, on the whole, seemed a more comfortable place for the lichen than for Zulma. Had she really hidden The Piggy there? And if so, why? I checked her vital statistics and found that her intelligence rating—IRSC—was only 10. The lichen's was 150. She had been bluffing, and was actually much *less* intelligent than the lichen! And so the poor idiot had hidden The Piggy on a planet where the lichen would be more comfortable than she was. I couldn't wait to get there.

I glanced back at the timer as Zena handed me the dice. The white part was now almost half covered by a semicircle of black. "Hey, it looks like an eclipse," I said.

"You got it, Barney. And at the instant of totality, you and your lovely little Mbridlengile will be blown to smithereens."

"Not if I can help it," I said. But things looked pretty grim. I was halfway across the board from Flaeioub, but Zulma now only had two stars to go—she'd be there for sure on the next move. Idiot though she was, she'd now have time to get The Piggy into her hand before I could reach it. Then I'd have to catch up with her before totality—and the shadow seemed to be moving ever more quickly across the timer's disk.

But I rolled only a 3. Hopelessly, I moved the lichen across three stars. They landed square in the middle of a black funnel.

"Oh, no, *now* what?" I groaned.

"But lichen, you're in luck," Zena said brightly. "You hit one of the hyperspace tunnels. Now you can go anywhere in the universe, instantly."

"On the same move?" I cried, hope rushing back.

"Instantly," she affirmed. It occurred to me that she didn't seem very upset by my good fortune, but I was too excited about entering hyperspace to think much about it. "Flaeioub, here I come!" I said, and plopped the lichen down in the center of the planet. "And now, the envelope, please," I demanded.

Zena rummaged through the black bag and produced the Flaeioub envelope. There were only two cards in it. The first one I pulled out, like all the others, was black on one side. The other side had a simple face drawn upon it, like the head of a stick figure. It was nothing but a circle containing a vapid, half-smiling mouth, and one wide-open eye, with a vertical iris like a cat's. But the single eye, and the unexpected crudeness of the drawing, gave me an unpleasant jolt. The ugly thing did not resemble a pig, but it was so pink and round, and so different from everything else in the game, that there was no doubt what it was. "I got it! I got The Piggy first!" I shouted at Zena.

"Don't count your offspring, lichen," Zena said quickly. "Hurry! Take out the other card."

The other card contained a wormlike, segmented thing, the carefully detailed shading giving it the three-dimensional quality of a scanning electron microscope photograph. "What is it?"

"*Lanthrococcus molluscans*," Zena said promptly. "A virulent bacteria, fatal to your species. By now, Flaeioub is permeated with it. It first attacks your digestive enzymes, so that you wither up, a helpless starving blob. After that, loathsome excrescences protrude agonizingly through your membranes." She smiled. "Too bad, lichen. You've had it."

"But—"

"Quick! The dice! Time's almost up!"

There was only a sliver of white on the timer. Zena rolled a 4, Zulma zoomed down to the surface of Flaeioub, and, using the special glasses she had carried with her, ripped The Piggy from the dry, crumbling mass that had once been the lichen.

The timer went black and emitted a piercing shriek. On the board, Mbridlengile flashed out of existence.

"But wait a minute! How come you didn't get killed by the bacteria?"

"Zulma had the vaccine, of course." She flashed a card. "See? She was immune."

"But what about the other creatures on Flaeioub. What did the bacteria do to them?"

"Sure, the gas bags that live there might get sick too." She shrugged. "But what was I expected to do? Sacrifice my own planet to protect *them*? Don't be absurd."

The disappointment I felt was not entirely due to having lost—which I had expected anyway. "Okay," I said, "But ... but wasn't it just chance that you got the bacteria *and* the vaccine? What kind of brilliant strategy is that? Anyone could win who happened to get those two cards."

"That's why it's superior to play with four instead of two. With four, the chance of getting a disease plus the vaccine is minimal. But it still isn't only chance. If you're clever enough, you can best someone who has almost anything. I'm afraid the lichen just didn't have the smarts."

I was insulted. "But the lichen **are** smarter than

Zulma," I argued. "Their intelligence was 150, and hers was only 10."

"The lower the IRSC number, the higher the intelligence, Barney. Interstellar Relative Sapience Code, it represents."

Suddenly I became aware of a peculiar sensation on my bare skin. I looked down. My shoulder was bright pink. "Oh, no!" I wailed, jumping to my feet. "Look how red my skin is already, and it's not even the next day yet! This is going to be the worst burn I've ever had in my life." I sloppily began pulling on my shirt.

"Don't overreact, Barney. That cream will guard you." She didn't sound very concerned.

"I better get inside now, anyway," I said, beginning to move away.

"Why don't you hold the rule book with you for a little while," she said. "We'll come and retrieve it when we need it. That way you might get a chance to catch up with us. We do want a fourth player. It's much more sensational than just three."

"Okay," I said, picking up the book. But now I wasn't thinking about the game. I was thinking about the document I had found in Zena's bedroom, which was still in my pocket. When would I get a chance to put it back, without being noticed? And when would I get a chance to find out anything about them, as I had planned to do today? The document was fascinating, but it didn't tell me who Zena and Manny and Joe were. I decided to plunge right in, as I had plunged headlong into the game. "Thanks," I said. "And thanks for letting me play. Uh . . . And I know you think I ask too many questions, but all three of you, you're so interesting, and unusual, and . . .

56

and you look like you spent more time than most people in the sun. We couldn't help being a little curious about what you do. I mean if you're doctors, or models, or what?"

She stared up at me in her white bikini. Her strong chin and heavy eyebrows gave a hint of masculinity to her face, all the more striking in contrast to her luscious body. She laughed. "Your curiosity is quite natural," she said. "You likely never have met anyone like us before, Barney. I imagine you could call us ... bons vivants. Playboys. We are all fortunate in that money has never been a serious issue for us." She raised her eyebrows; they emphasized her words like two dark exclamation marks. "Nothing has. We are able to do whatever we like doing."

"But if you could do anything, go anywhere, then why come here?" I paused, my shirt half on. "I mean this is kind of a run-down, nature reserve beach area. Why not go someplace more exclusive?"

"For a change, Barney. We've been to the exclusive ones. We've met those people. At times you need a change. Even a primitive minor dump like this cottage can be an interesting experience, if you don't feel the drawbacks too seriously." She lifted her chin. "We try not to feel anything too seriously."

"Except for your tans," I quipped, aware of my skin again.

"That's right, Barney." She lay back on the towel. "Our tans are serious business."

Your tans and your games, I thought, heading back toward our house. Why didn't I believe her? Her explanation made a certain kind of sense—more sense than the crazy ideas Mom and Dad had about them. Who else but wealthy playboys could afford to devote so much energy to those empty pursuits? There had been little evidence at their house that they had any other serious interests.

Except for the document. The document that had brought them here, purposefully, to search our house. That search had been very serious indeed, so serious that their personalities had changed; so important to them that they had forgotten everything else.

Especially when they had been examining my room, and the scratch marks on the walls.

6

I shut the door of my room, flung myself onto the bed, pulled the document out of my pocket, and began to read.

Again, weeping overcame him. I pushed him aside with an oath and tore the bedclothes from the shape beneath. And there I beheld an apparition so ghastly that my senses reeled, and I did swoon against the bedpost, blotting out the vision with my two trembling hands.

A moment later I bared my eyes, and beheld—merely the body of a strangled man. Black and hideous of countenance it was, yes, with staring eyes and distended tongue. And yet not what I had seen—or imagined I had seen—at first impression.

It had been a false vision, my first impression, the product of my overwrought condition, and of my brother's hysterical utterance—of that I am now convinced. For what I had thought to be a coarse leathery, greenish, *reptilian* hide was indeed only a man's flesh ravaged by the elements and the unnatural manner of his death; and what in horror I had perceived against all reason as some *invertebrate* organism, gelatinous, sluglike, protruding from the cracked, blackened lips, that in my swoon had appeared actually to writhe in a most grisly and somehow *beckoning* manner—I quail now at the very memory—was in truth merely his deformed and swollen tongue; and most ghastly of all, the *third* eye, the yet living eye, that had appeared to *wink* from the folds of his forehead, yellow and filmed with slime—'twas not but a bruise, a swollen *contusion* of the struggle, partially obscured by matted hair. Nothing, nothing but that.

"The Devil, Tobias, can you not see? It was *fate* that brought him to me, and I could only do what I have done," gasped my brother, weeping.

"It is not only fate, my dear Ethan, but how a man *responds* to the blows dealt him by fate, that determines his true destiny," I spoke, my rage abated, my grief only commencing to flower.

And though to keelhaul a man is indeed a cruel and unusual punishment if any there be, yet it could not be by *my* hand that my own flesh and blood should actually be put to death. And so it was done. Yet even as Ethan was pushed from the bow, he continued to maintain, with the utmost conviction, that the false vision was in fact the truth.

And, taking pity, I did not give orders to wrest from him the trinket, which it appeared he had taken from his victim's garment and which seemed to give him some comfort. I could see no harm in it, an ornament perhaps, to which he clung so desperately, to which he clung even as he was pulled from the water, to which he *still* clings. . . .

I let the papers fall from my hand, staring at the marks around the windows. It was just about the grimmest thing I had ever read. And it felt very odd to be lying in the very room in which Ethan had spent the rest of his life. What had it been like to be locked in this room for twenty years?

I got up, feeling like an idiot, and checked the door to make sure I wasn't locked in.

The strangest thing about the document was the captain's hallucination. For a moment, he had seen what his simpleminded brother had imagined—a three-eyed creature with a greenish hide and a slug in his mouth. What did the captain's vision really mean? I couldn't figure it out.

There was one thing I was sure about: Despite the relaxed impression Zena was trying to make, the neighbors' interest in the captain's story wasn't trivial at all. But what were the three of them looking for? Whatever it was, they hadn't found it in the house this morning. And where else was there to look?

I was a little drowsy from all the sun that afternoon. As I lay there, my eyes kept returning to the markings on the wall. And perhaps they did form a sort of pattern after all, like the spokes of a lopsided wheel. The lines were spaced in such a way that they did seem to radiate from some point within one of the windows. Yet the generalized halo they formed around the rectangle of glass was not symmetrical. The angles between the lines varied, as though the point from which they sprang was not in the exact middle of the window, but toward the bottom and off to the side. And perhaps they were not shooting out from this off-center spot at all. Perhaps they were rushing toward it, zeroing in on some focal point in the glass. Or some important location in the view *beyond* the window. . . .

I sat up and rubbed my eyes. I told myself I was imagining things. They were the random scratches of a madman. There was no way they could be precise enough to indicate any one particular spot in the landscape. The way they seemed to focus in so neatly toward a single point was an illusion, like one of those psychological tricks of perception in which straight lines appear to be curved. My brain was deluding me, trying to make sense where there was none. It was like the captain's sympathetic hallucination, a product of his brother's power of suggestion. And now the maniac was trying to fool me as well!

I lay down again and tried to doze. But the scratch marks wouldn't let me escape, burning against the blackness of my eyelids. The only way I was going to get them off my mind was to *prove* that they were not all pointing at the same spot. I dazedly tried to convince myself that if the pattern were that obvious, someone else would have noticed before now. But that wasn't good enough. I was going to have to demonstrate it for myself, once and for all.

In the kitchen I found a ball of twine and cut off a three-foot length. I got a roll of tape and borrowed a pink felt-tipped pen from Mom's purse. I stood beside the window and taped the string to the end of a scratch mark. I stretched it along the mark and across the window, and drew a faint line on the glass with the pink pen. I pulled off the tape, selected another scratch mark, and repeated the process.

The two lines crossed directly over a large boulder at the southern tip of the island.

But that didn't prove anything. Almost any two random lines would cross somewhere on the window. I picked another scratch mark and drew another line.

The three lines intersected neatly at the same spot.

It had to be a coincidence. All I was doing was wasting my time and making a mess on the glass. The only sensible thing to do was to stop immediately and wipe off the glass. But I couldn't stop. I drew a fourth line, a fifth, a sixth. My hands were sweating, but I didn't notice. I drew ten lines, fifteen lines, oblivious to everything but the web of pink slowly forming its relentless pattern across the foam-flecked bay, the fat clouds, the small, steeply sloped island.

And every line met at precisely the same point.

"Barney, what are you doing?"

I dropped the pen and spun around. Mom was wearing her skirted, one-piece pink-flowered suit, and her skin tone had deepened from bubble gum to puce.

"I was just . . . I don't . . ." I explained.

"But just *look* at the mess you've made! Like a baby. How do you think you're going to get that off?" She squinted at it. "What is it, anyway? It looks like geometry."

"It's just . . . an idea I had."

"An idea?"

"Well, you know, it has to do with that story about the house, about the captain who—"

"You sound feverish. Let me feel your forehead." She started toward me, her hand lifted, her eyes on the window.

"No, I'm fine," I said, stretching out my hands to protect the window.

"Let me clean it. You can make your little drawings on a piece of paper. Let me—"

"No, no, I'll clean it later," I said, backing against the window. "It'll come off real easy. I tested it first," I lied.

She tried to edge around me, her hand reaching for the glass. "Will you please get out of the way? If I can't get it clean, we'll have to pay them for a new window. I don't suppose you thought of that, did you?"

"I'll clean it, I told you!" I insisted and spun around to face the window. Next door, I saw then, the men had just returned. Plastic surfboards and poles were piled beside the car. All three neighbors were standing on the lawn, motionless. Joe was pointing out across the water—it looked, in fact, as though he was pointing directly at the large boulder on the southern tip of the island—and there was an eagerness in the way they were all staring at the island, like beasts of prey tensed to pounce.

Then Mom nudged me out of the way with her shoulder. A second later she was busy with both hands.

"No! Don't!"

"Paper towels and window cleaner, that's what it's going to take," she said. "I just hope I can get this mess off my hands." She studied her palms, clucking her teeth. Nothing was left of my neat and perfect design but a big pink smear.

"Oh, now you've ruined it," I sighed, and sank down onto the bed. But it didn't matter. I knew where the lines were pointing.

The problem now was to figure out how to get out there first.

7

I woke up the next morning with the worst sunburn of my entire life.

It was not a mere uncomfortable reddening of the skin. It was a disease. The symptoms were headache, fever, nausea, and pain so intense that the thin cotton sheet had become a hot iron molded to the contours of my body. Before I knew what was happening, I was moaning with such wretched and uncontrolled abandon that the sound woke Mom.

"Poor Barney," she kept saying, as she wrung out washcloths for my forehead and hovered over me with a can of anesthetic spray, which had no noticeable effect. "You know how sensitive you are to the sun."

"I just didn't think about the time, that's all," I whined. "Ow! Don't touch me there!"

"But it's not like you. Something must have made you forget. Why won't you tell me?"

I didn't know why I wouldn't tell her; I only knew I wanted to keep Interstellar Pig a secret between myself and the neighbors for the time being. "I went for a walk on the beach," I lamely explained. "It was pretty. I forgot how long I was out."

"But you couldn't get away from the beach fast enough when you came down with us. What made you go back for so long when we *weren't* there?"

"Because there's nothing else to *do* in this stupid place but go to the beach!" I said, my voice rising.

"But you hate the beach!"

"Then why did you take me to the beach?" I screamed at her.

"Don't talk to me like that! It's not like you." She sounded close to tears. "You make it sound like it's *my* fault you did this thing to yourself, and I'm only trying to make you feel better."

"I'm sorry. I'm all right, I can take care of myself, okay?" I forced a smile, feeling guilty. She pouted back at me. "Just, go work on your tan while the weather's good," I said. "That's what you're here for. Now's your chance. It might rain for the rest of the week."

"Are you sure you'll be all right, dear?" she said, all solicitude. But she couldn't prevent her eyes from darting to the window to check for clouds.

Miserable as I was, I almost laughed. "I'll be all right," I insisted, reaching for the rule book. "I feel like reading. I just got to the good part."

She left me alone at last. But I couldn't concentrate for long on the rule book; the information was too complicated to distract me from pain. For a time I just lay there in the stifling little room feeling sorry for myself and trying to blame everything on Zena. But that didn't help much, since I knew it was really my own fault. Yes, she had pressured me to stay out in the sun with her. But I could have insisted on staying inside, or at least on protecting myself better.

And when was she going to notice the document missing from her drawer? And how was I going to return it?

At the moment, the three of them seemed to be having breakfast on the patio. I lay there listening vaguely to their boisterous voices, which were audible even from upstairs.

"Ugh! You let the milk go sour again, Manny," Zena groaned. "Can't you learn to recollect the date?"

"Sour? A little *mûr*, maybe. But what difference could that make to you, the way you keep piling the raw onions on your bagel at *breakfast*? It must be murder on your taste buds; they're probably covered with scar tissue. No surprise you oversalt everything."

"On the contrary, Manny. It invigorates them, like exercising your muscles. I'm not a little fragile delicate creature like you; I like to be stimulated in the morning. Especially when you give me this flavorless swill you name coffee. I don't know how you can put this crummy milk in it; black, it's bland as dishwater."

"What did I tell you? You can't taste anything anymore. It's sad, that's what it is. A mad, hopeless, frenzied quest for sensation. You know it can only lead to one end. If you weren't so irritating, I'd pity you."

"Stop it!" There was a clatter of silverware on the cement. "It's too early in the morning to tolerate your prissy superiority. And Joe likes his coffee stronger too. When *he* makes it, it tastes like something. Isn't that right, Joe? Well? Isn't it?"

"Typical. You know you're wrong, so you drag in somebody else to bolster you up."

I sat up and began listening more closely. Their voices were different today, nervy, high-strung. Their banter wasn't boisterous; it was as sour as Manny's old milk.

"Well, I do like it a little stronger." Joe's voice was quieter, conciliatory. "So from now on we concoct it a little stronger and Manny puts more milk in his. That's no problem. The problem is, if you two don't stop bickering and finish eating, we'll never get going while the tide's still high. I don't want to run aground halfway out to the island."

I was out of bed and at the window, craning my head out. The three windsurfer boards were laid out on the lawn. Joe had risen from the table and was moving toward the cottage with plate and mug in his hands. "Come on, bring the breakfast stuff inside," he said.

So they were actually going out to the island on those funny surfboard things with sails. Had they already interpreted the marks around the window? At this point there was no way of knowing. What I did know was that I couldn't let them get to the island without me.

I tried to argue with myself as I struggled, whimpering, into my clothes. But I really didn't have any choice. They had come here to look for something relating to the document, that was obvious. They hadn't found it in the house. The only other information that existed, the marks around the window, pointed directly at the boulder on the island. If they got there and found what they were looking for, they'd just leave, without telling me anything. I'd never learn the whole story, I'd never know what the three of them were really after. I had to find it—whatever it was—before they did. And that meant getting out to the island, however miserable the prospect seemed to me now.

The blue jeans and long-sleeved sweat shirt I wore were horribly itchy and hot, but necessary. I even put on a stupid plastic visor Mom had bought for me which I had never worn before. She and Dad had already left for someone's private beach, and I slammed out the door and raced over to the cottage without even planning a strategy. The three neighbors, in swimsuits and nylon backpacks, were just stepping onto the lawn as I arrived.

"*Mein Gott,* what happened to you?" said Joe.

"Ooh, it hurts just to *look* at you!" Manny said with a shudder.

"Poor Barney!" Zena made a hissing sound through her teeth. "Don't inform me you got that burn yesterday, with me."

I nodded. "Does it really look that horrible?"

"Like a boiled lobster," Manny said. "Hey, why don't we have lobster for dinner tonight!"

Zena moved close beside me, biting her lower lip as she stared down at my face. "Oh, Barney, I just didn't comprehend. And after you *told* me how sensitive you were! Oh, God, it's all my fault!"

Manny shook his head and pressed his lips together. "I can just see it," he said. "You *made* him sit outside with you, even though he told you he couldn't absorb the sun. Typical."

She ignored him. "Oh, I'm so penitent, Barney. But it was after two, and you did put that cream on. . . ." She bit

69

her lip again. "Oh, if only there was something I could do!" she cried with exaggerated hysteria. "I mean it. I'd do anything to atone for what happened."

"Oh, that's okay, it wasn't—" I began. Then I saw that Joe had picked up one of the windsurfers and was carrying it toward the car. I began to have an idea. "Except that, well, maybe there *is* something you could do...."

"What is it, Barney? A salve? An anesthetic? *I* know! I have some marvelous painkillers. They're in my drawer, somewhere." She turned toward the house.

"No, nothing like that," I said quickly. "But there is something I would like."

"Yeah?" she said, her voice becoming businesslike. "Out with it."

"Uh, Zena, we're kind of in a hurry," Manny said, edging away from us.

"It's those windsurfers. I've always dreamed of going on one of them, ever since I first saw one," I lied. The idea of putting my body on one of the contraptions seemed as much fun as jumping out of an airplane. "Could you, maybe, take me for a ride? That would be great!"

"Certainly, Barney," she said briskly. "We're going out to the island today, but we could take you out tomorrow. We borrowed them for a couple of days."

"Oh, I'd love to go out to the island!" I said. "Couldn't I go with you today?"

"Today? You want to go out to the island with us today?" Frowning, she glanced over at the others, who had finished loading the boards into the car. "Gee, Barney, that might kind of helix up our plans."

"Oh, *please*," I said, hating to beg, but seeing no alternative. "Ever since we came here, I've been staring out at the island and wishing I could sail out there. It would just mean so much. And ... and tomorrow I can't go."

She looked impatient now.

Manny seemed worried. "But we really couldn't, could we?" he said, turning his head back and forth between me and Joe.

They didn't want me on the island because they didn't want me to know they were looking for something there. Which meant that my best tactic was to make them think they were safer taking me along than leaving me behind. ...

"If you can't go tomorrow, we'll take you out the next day," Joe was saying. "We'll take you out all day, every day, for the next week. But today won't manage. See you later."

"We're in a hurry now, Barney," Zena said. "And with that burn you can't go out today anyway."

"Yes, I can," I said, thinking fast. "Dad did ask me if I wanted to go with them on Ted's motorboat. We can follow you and watch you with his superpowerful binoculars all day. That might be fun."

"What!" Manny cried.

There was a brief stunned silence, during which they all watched each other. Then Zena said, "Well, on twice thought, uh ... Do you think ... could we attempt it, Joe?"

Now Manny was smirking at her. "Zena and her clever little gambits," he said and rolled his eyes.

"Shut up, Manny!" Joe said. But he was glaring at Zena too. Then he coughed and smiled weakly in my direction, playing with his mustache. "You didn't inform them we were going to the island, did you?"

"How could I? I didn't know. But now I'll tell them. We can *all* go out to the island with you. They said they'd take me anywhere I wanted."

"Well ... perhaps you could come with us, Barney. If we hurry," Joe said.

"You win, Barney," Zena said, sour and ungracious and also somewhat suspicious. "Since it's so terribly important to you." She turned abruptly away. "Come on, *vamos!*"

"Who's he going to ride with?" Manny asked.

"Not me," Zena said. "My board's too small."

"Well, not me, either," Manny said. "I'm so bad at it anyway. A passenger would slow me down. I'd never even get there."

"Joe should take him," Zena announced. "He's the best one at, uh ... *aquatic* activities. Confess it, Joe."

"That's right," Manny said. "Joe's the best. He should take him."

"Hey, now wait a minute," Joe protested. "How did all this ... ?" He looked at me, shaking his head as though trying to come up with another excuse to get rid of me. Then he grunted. "Sure, I'll take him," he said, sliding into the driver's seat and slamming the door. He shot a glance at Manny and Zena. "Even with a passenger, I'll still be miles ahead of you two."

We bumped down to the beach. I paced at the water's edge, trying to keep the exposed parts of my body in my own shadow as the others unrolled their sails and shoved them into the holes in the middle of the boards. The other people windsurfing on the bay were tipping over more than they were staying up, I noticed with some trepidation, even though the water was calm and there seemed to be little wind.

"How come everybody keeps tipping over?" I asked, following behind Joe as they pushed the boards out into the water. It was the first time I had ventured in, and though it was the bay and not the ocean, I would have liked it a bit warmer. I wished I could have eased in slowly, but the three of them were in a hurry. Standing on tiptoe only prolonged the agony; I gasped as the water hit my stomach.

"Everybody overturns a lot at first," Manny called out to me.

"Manny overturns a lot *all* the time," Zena said.

"Oh, shut up!" he shouted, and splashed her.

Some of the spray hit my face and I winced away. "But do *you* tip over a lot?" I asked Joe. Of the three of them, he was the one I felt least comfortable with.

"Naw, not in this little breeze," he reassured me. He climbed onto the board, stood up swaying, planted his feet firmly apart, and began dragging the sail up out of the water. "Slide onto the board on your stomach and hang on," he commanded.

My stomach was one of the most sensitive areas. And the hard plastic board, it turned out, was not smooth but textured like sandpaper, presumably to keep the sailor's feet from slipping. Even with my sweat shirt on, sliding across the thing would be torture. I delicately draped my chest over the back and rested my hands underneath, pushing up my sleeves to try to keep them dry.

The board rocked as Joe began fighting with the wildly whipping sail. "You must get up out of the water, Barney, or I'll never get this thing under control," he ordered me, grunting. "Come on, *move*. Slide up on it."

I obeyed, and groaned as the textured board scraped

against me. Joe didn't seem to hear. He was still working at getting the sail adjusted, swearing under his breath and scowling. None of them wanted me on this journey, least of all him. I was the outsider, pitiful, uninvited. I hated it; the psychological pain was worse than the physical. Could I really tolerate it for an entire day? What was I getting myself into?

But I didn't have time to brood about it now. The sail snapped into position and filled with wind. Joe stopped staggering on the board, his feet rooted in place, his widely spaced hands grasping the curved boom. He leaned backward, suddenly graceful, his body balanced against the wind. "Get your feet out of the water!" he yelled at me. I made one final, wrenching effort, dragging myself forward until my face was almost touching his foot. We were off.

I clung desperately to the board, rigid with tension, prepared at any moment to be thrown off. But as we continued to move, gaining speed, it began to dawn on me that my position was not as precarious as I was trying to make it. The board held steady as it skimmed over the bay, smooth and secure, silent except for the lapping of the waves. There was something serene about the sensation, especially since I didn't have to do anything but lie there.

I risked a quick glance behind to see how the others were doing. Manny was in the water, struggling to extricate himself from his wet sail. Zena's long limbs were splayed awkwardly and her behind jutted out, but she was at least upright and moving forward. The beach was a thin strip behind them, the sunbathers already faceless with distance.

"Don't jerk, Barney, I'm coming about!" Joe shouted as I turned back. He edged quickly around the mast and let the wind whip the sail to the other side of the board. We now seemed to be heading directly for the island. A moment later he looked quickly down at me. "Just relax," he said condescendingly. "We're making good progress. Nothing to be afraid of."

"I'm not afraid," I told him, insulted, though only minutes before I'd been terrified. "I like it. It's fun. Good thing I came with you, though."

"The good thing is, I carried the food," he said. "But they'll do all right, once they get the sensation of it again. They'll attain the island one of these days."

We didn't speak much for the rest of the trip. My neck began to ache from craning it forward to see where we were going, so I just rested my head on the board and stared at Joe's feet. They were wide and bumpy and calloused, and there were funny purplish stains under his toenails. Had their last expedition been a grape crushing tour of Italy?

Though Joe maintained control of the board, my feeling of serenity didn't last. Soon my back began to ache from the constant effort of keeping my legs out of the water. But every time I tried to change position, Joe yelled at me to stop jerking. I did manage to let go with one hand long enough to see that the underside of my arm, which had not been burned, was covered with tiny little welts from the textured surface of the board. How far away was the island anyway? I wasn't going to be able to hold on much longer. I was a lousy swimmer, but I could always just float on my back until someone came to save me. My clothes were soaked through, my behind itched miserably, and I began to shiver. I clenched my teeth to keep them from chattering. I stifled the whimper that kept wanting to crawl from my throat. Could I manage to hold on for five minutes longer? For one minute? If I let go, I would probably drown, but maybe that wouldn't be so bad. Nothing could be worse than this.

My arms began to loosen, the strength drained out of them. And Joe said, "Watch it, Barney. The sail's coming down. We made it."

I slipped off with a sigh, and my hands and knees sank into the sandy bottom. I waded to the beach and watched Joe dismantle the board.

Then it hit me. This beach was deserted. There was not another person in sight. It was an odd sensation to be so isolated, and I wasn't sure I liked it. But suddenly I felt elated. I had done something that yesterday had seemed impossible. I had made it to the island before the three of them had had a chance to explore it. And I knew just where to start to search.

Then I looked beyond the beach, and my elation vanished. The island was completely different. From my window I had seen a long narrow strip of beach encircling a low wooded hill with one very clear, rocky outcropping at which the marks pointed. But now I was standing on a wide strip of beach that ended at a very steep, almost clifflike, hillside that I wasn't even sure I could climb, and I could see no rocky outcropping at all, no large boulder. I turned back to the mainland again, searching for our house to see what part of the island the windows faced. But from this distance I could see many tiny houses scattered along the coastline, and they all looked the same. I couldn't even tell where our beach was.

Then Joe cursed, and stumbled in the shallow water.

"What's the matter?" I shouted.

"Something bit me." He limped up onto the beach, dragging the windsurfer behind him. He sat down heavily on the sand. I hurried over to him. A crab was clinging to his purplish big toe.

"The ignorant little thing should have known better," Joe snarled. He pulled the crab from his foot. With surprising brutality, he crushed the shell in his large hand, then hurled the still wriggling mess into the water. He ripped the pack from his back and pulled out a box of bandages. "Slow me down, all right," he muttered to himself. "Good thing they're so far behind."

I looked back over the water. Zena and Manny, who kept tipping over, seemed only about halfway to the island. It occurred to me that this was my chance to start trying to find the boulder before they did.

"You need any help?" I asked Joe timidly.

"I can take care of myself, thanks."

"Listen, uh, I have to go back into the woods," I said.

"Huh? What for?" he said, concentrating on the gash on his foot, which was still bleeding.

"Call of nature," I said, backing away.

"Don't go too far," he said. "If you're not back soon, we'll eat all the food up. You know how greedy Zena is."

"I'm not hungry," I said, still retreating.

"Avoid the southern part of the island," he warned, squinting up at me. "I hear there's quicksand there, and a treacherous undertow."

"Okay," I said, and turned and hurried away. I looked back once and he was staring after me. Was he suspicious? He certainly didn't want me to get anywhere near the southern tip of the island, where the boulder was. It was to the left, I knew that much, but naturally I didn't want him to see me go that way. I just headed directly up the hillside, into the trees. My hope was that if I got high enough, I might be able to get a view of the whole island, and that way find the exact location of the boulder I had seen from my window.

I followed a steep sandy path that gradually became covered with pine needles as the trees thickened around me. The beach was out of sight now, and I began to wonder whether Zena and Manny had arrived and how soon they would start looking. There were three of them, after all; they could split up and cover the island three times as fast as I could. I didn't have much time. I began to run. The path leveled off, which seemed to indicate that I had reached the top of the hill. But I couldn't see anything because of the trees. The island was turning out to be much larger than I had expected. I began to get frantic. Should I leave the path? What would happen if I got lost? Would they leave without me? Was there really any quicksand? When were the trees going to end?

The path wound off to the right, but the trees seemed thinner to the left. But was the southern tip of the island still to my left? My sense of direction had never been very good. If I went the wrong way and ended up blundering around on the northern side of the island, I'd never find the place before they did. But I couldn't just keep on thrashing around in the trees, getting nowhere. I had to make a decision. I stopped, cursing. I hated decisions. What was the matter with me, anyway? Not only was I making a pest of myself, I was probably destroying my skin. And for what? I didn't even know what I was trying to find.

I stopped thinking and plunged off to the left. There was underbrush here that scratched my bare feet. I was sweating and the visor kept slipping down over my forehead. I now had no idea in which direction I was going or even where the path had been. And I was too stupid and confused to think of getting my direction from the sun.

But I was lucky. The woods began to thin out. Now there was sand beneath my feet instead of needles. And suddenly I emerged from the trees and found myself at the top of a steep dune, staring directly down at a long pointed strip of beach. Finally it looked familiar. This was the southern tip of the island that I saw from my window. To my right were low bushes and more hills of sand sloping gradually down to the water.

I spun around to the left and there it was, a huge granite boulder poking up out of the trees. It was only a few dozen yards away and easily recognizable. In minutes I was standing at the base of it, at the exact focus of the marks around the window. I couldn't see the house, but somehow I could feel a presence, as though I had been swept back a hundred years and the demented prisoner was staring out at me from the little room. . . .

I wasn't being fanciful. The captain's brother had brought me here, as directly as if he had led me by the hand. But what for? What was I supposed to do now? The boulder was twenty feet high and covered with gray green lichen, devoid of footholds, too steep to climb. There was no cave in which to hide anything, no message carved in the rock, no secret passageway. I felt like throwing myself down on the ground and crying like a baby.

But before I did that, I just happened to walk around behind the boulder, where there was a little sandy knoll among the trees, protected from the wind. And there I found a tumbled down pile of rotten timbers that must have once been a primitive shack or lean-to. And buried under the boards I discovered the battered trunk, not locked, but with hinges so rusty that I had to bang it with a rock before I could get it open. And inside it, a small object, some kind of tarnished metal box.

It was exactly like *Treasure Island* or "The Gold Bug." The marks on my bedroom wall were the map, pointing to the treasure that could have been hidden here over one hundred years ago. The object itself, I had to admit, seemed unprepossessing at first glance. But maybe the real treasure was hidden inside the rusty little box. I knew there had to be something important about it.

"Hey, look! There's Joe, over to the right." It was Manny's voice, coming from the woods.

"He's limping. Hey, Joe! We're overtaking you after all!" Zena cried shrilly.

"But I'll get there first, anyway," Joe called back, panting. His voice was alarmingly close. I could hear the rustle and crunch of underbrush now as they plowed toward me through the trees.

I covered the empty trunk with boards and stood up. I got out of the clearing and raced around to the front of the boulder, clutching the object. They hadn't come the way I had, so all I had to do to get away from them was to run the few dozen yards along the top of the dune and then dart back into the trees at the same spot at which I had emerged only minutes before.

They were fast, faster than I had expected. While I had been wasting time wandering stupidly around in the woods, they had zeroed in on the exact spot.

"Here's the boulder! I discovered it!" Zena cried, with frantic excitement.

"Hey, no fair kicking!" Manny squealed.

"I saw it first!"

"But I'll *get* there first!"

I hurried away from them into the trees. But I *found* it first, I called silently after them. I had little trouble retracing my steps, and got back to the landing place on the beach before they did. I worked out a plausible story about getting lost in the woods on the northern end of the island. And I didn't make the mistake of sitting around and staring at the little box while I was out in the open and there was even the slightest chance they might see me. I shoved it into the pocket of my jeans.

They hadn't even touched the food.

8

I had thought the ride out to the island was uncomfortable, but it was luxurious compared to the trip back.

All three of them were in a rotten mood when they returned. They asked me desultorily where I had been, and they *seemed* to believe my story about getting lost on the other end of the island. After that they made no effort to be sociable, but just sat around glaring at each other until the tide was high enough again to start back.

But the weather had changed. The water was choppy and the wind kept shifting. Even Joe had trouble controlling his board. It thrashed and pitched and scraped my arms horribly, Joe kept shouting at me to stop rocking it, as though the weather were my fault, and we capsized several times in the middle of the bay. The water was like ice. I was shivering so helplessly that I could barely hold on to the board.

Still, *I* had found the treasure first, before they had. However miserable I was now, I could look forward to examining it at leisure in my room when the day was over.

Or so I tried to tell myself as I came limping and shivering into our house. There were cooking noises coming from the kitchen. I made a rush for the stairs, hoping at least to get into dry clothes before Mom got a look at me, but she was too fast. "Barney, you're soaking wet! And with that burn!"

I had made it to the landing. "I'm not really wet . . . and I'm not cold at all," I said, through blue lips and chattering teeth.

"Well, I think it might have been wiser to wait until your burn was better before going off with those people on an all-day outing."

She must have seen me riding back in the neighbors' car. "It's just that they had to go out to the island today," I said, truthfully. "And I really wanted to see what it was like out there. It was my only chance."

"Oh, and look at all the sand you've tracked in," Mom said.

Dad laughed. "There's no way to keep sand out of a beach house," he said. "What was the island like, Barney? It's supposed to be one of the most isolated wildlife sanctuaries in the area. See anything interesting?"

"I guess all the animals were hiding from us," I said. "Maybe we made too much noise."

"Did you learn any more about them?" Mom asked me eagerly. She glanced at Dad. "Too bad we went out so early—we could have gone with them too. I'm sure those two young men knew all about wildlife. They have the look of . . . of forest rangers, or something," she added dreamily.

Mom had never before shown the slightest interest in wildlife.

"She does seem to be having a good influence on Barney," Dad said, watching me with a peculiar half smile. "Er, I mean, they *all* do. Getting him interested in nature."

"Well, I just hope you're not pushing yourself at the neighbors," Mom said. "After all, they're sophisticated adults, and I'm sure they know everyone who matters in this area. They told us yesterday that they have scads of invitations. So it's very kind of them to include you, but you mustn't be a pest."

"I'm sure Barney isn't a pest, but he should be aware that people with their responsibilities can't just play all the time," Dad said. "They probably have a lot of important work to do, even on vacation."

"But they don't," I argued. "The only thing they care about is—"

Mom interrupted me as though I didn't know what I was talking about. "All we're saying is, Barney, that you mustn't be hurt if sometimes they want to get rid of you. After all, they're *so much* older than you."

"No, they're not," I said. How had Mom and Dad managed to pick up such a completely unreal picture of the neighbors? "They're hardly more than college age."

Mom smiled knowledgeably. "Well, that's very generous of you, Barney. Now you take a hot shower and get some dry clothes on before dinner." She started for the kitchen.

Upstairs I peeled off my clothes and headed quickly for the shower, too chilled and shivering for the moment to take a good look at the object I had found, whatever it was. I was proud of myself for finding it first, but also felt slightly guilty. After all, the creased and faded document proved that the neighbors had been looking for it for a while, and it was a little unfair that I should suddenly come along and whisk it out from under their noses.

Of course, I could always just give it to them, if it turned out to be rightfully theirs. But I wasn't going to do that right away, I decided. I'd keep it long enough at least to find out what it was, and why they wanted it so much. And I could take my time, because I was pretty sure they had no idea that I had it. If they had suspected that, they would certainly have tried to get it away from me back on the island, and they had almost totally ignored me.

The one thing that did worry me was endangering my friendship with them by being so pushy today. I had to make up for it somehow, and get back in their good graces again. It wasn't just that they were the only interesting people around, and I'd be bored without them. There was also a powerful attraction about them that was difficult to explain. I just knew, somehow, that I wanted them to like me, very much indeed.

I was fortunate, in any case, that Mom and Dad did not object to my spending so much time with older people, as I would have expected them to. Perhaps their lenience had something to do with the image the neighbors were able to project. They made a good impression on everybody, it seemed—another useful skill they had perfected.

And yet it was more than just a good impression, I thought, as I gingerly dried myself. The picture they created of themselves seemed to differ, depending on the observer. Mom and Dad thought the neighbors were their own age. Mom was not only uncharacteristically attracted to them, but she also assumed they knew all the "important" people. Dad had the idea that they had some kind of vital role to play in the world, and so he found them interesting and impressive. What Mom and Dad saw in the neighbors, it seemed, was precisely what each of them *wanted* to see.

I stood naked in my room, the towel hanging from my hand. And what about myself? Was I also seeing some kind of unreal image of them? Was that what their attraction was?

And if so, what was the reality underneath?

"Barney! Dinner!"

I dropped the towel and angrily pulled open a drawer. I was getting carried away by the captain's bizarre story, by the imaginary intricacies of Interstellar Pig. The neighbors were exceptionally winning people, and exceptionally rich. It was only natural that people would want to like them, and be liked in return. And I certainly hadn't been under any kind of delusion when I had seen how sullen and quarrelsome they could be today, when things didn't go exactly as they wanted. As for Mom and Dad, they probably needed glasses.

I picked up my wet pants, to make sure the little box was there.

"Your dinner's getting cold, Barney!"

I felt the box through the cloth, then draped the pants over the chair. I would have to wait until after dinner to examine it carefully.

But even then I didn't get a chance. We had barely finished eating when Manny came to the door, telling Mom how delicious everything smelled, exclaiming with delight over a bite of her Grape-Nut pudding, then remembering to mention that he had come to pick up a book I had borrowed. "And maybe Barney's ready for a four-man game—that is, if he has your permission to leave before the dishes are done. We'd really have to start right away or there wouldn't be time."

I dashed upstairs to get the rule book. I had time only to slip the little box out of my wet pants and hide it at the bottom of a drawer.

"I hope you don't think we're monopolizing him," Manny was explaining when I came down. "If you've known any bridge addicts, you'll understand. You've just got to have that fourth player—and Zena says Barney does seem to have an aptitude for the game."

Both Mom and Dad were staring rather foolishly at Manny, like infatuated teenagers. I felt embarrassed for them and uncomfortable. Were these really my normal, ordinary parents? Manny must think they were a pair of dopes.

"What kind of game is it?" Dad finally asked.

"Oh, it's kind of a science fiction adventure game," Manny explained, edging for the door.

"I guess it must help you to relax, unwind, get your minds off more important things," Dad suggested.

"Why don't you all come over here for a snack or a drink or something when the game is over?" Mom said, nearly panting with eagerness.

"That's very sweet of you, but I can't promise for the others," Manny said. "The game can be rather draining."

"Well then be back by ten," Mom said to me, sounding miffed—she actually seemed to be jealous! "I don't want you getting overtired and catching cold."

"We'll build a big fire and *drown* him in hot chocolate,"

Manny said. "And we promise to throw him out on the dot of ten, even if the game isn't over. Come on, amigo." Beaming warmly, he held the door open for me.

I was so relieved at being back in their good graces that I didn't stop to wonder why, after treating me like an unwanted pest all afternoon, they should already, this quickly, be so eager for my company. And what about the frustration and disappointment they must be feeling about not finding the object of their painstaking search? Didn't it occur to me that their sudden ebullience, in face of *that*, was a shade suspicious?

It didn't. What occurred to me was that they were dying for a four-handed game of Interstellar Pig. And so was I.

9

Zena, by some coincidence, once again drew Zulma, the brilliant and hideous spider-lady from Vavoosh.

Manny drew Moyna, one of the octopuslike gas bag creatures from Flaeioub, with an IRSC of 22.9. It was this species that Zena had so casually infected with *Lanthrococcus molluscans* in the last game, and I kind of hoped that now Manny would pay her back.

Joe drew Jrlb, a water-breathing gill man from Thrilb, who looked like a swordfish with rudimentary arms and legs and had an IRSC of 16.

And I drew Luap, a sapient reptile from Ja-Ja-Bee, the ice planet. I was glad to see that he was humanoid in appearance, except for his leathery green hide and three eyes. He also had a symbiotic relationship with a sluglike invertebrate that lived inside his mouth. He was oxygen-breathing, but couldn't remain for long in temperatures much over 32 degrees Fahrenheit or his blood would boil. His IRSC was a depressing 25.

There was something gnawingly familiar about Luap, and I wondered vaguely which science fiction novel had included a creature similar to him. But once the game got going, I stopped thinking about it.

And it certainly was another game from the simple-minded two-handed version I had played with Zena, in which both players always knew who had The Piggy. Now, any of the other three might have it, if you didn't. How on earth did you go about figuring out which one it was? I had no idea and would have been a goner before the game even began.

Only, I had The Piggy.

It was a fantastic stroke of luck. Even so, the sight of that pink face with its one eye made me gulp queasily. Why did it have to be so ugly?

I did my best to check out the atmospheres and temperatures of the various planets, without being too obvious about it. Flaeioub, Vavoosh and Thrilb were out of the question as hiding places for The Piggy, being the comfortable home planets of the other players. I hardly dared hide it on my own planet of Ja-Ja-Bee, even though they'd be frozen solid there and I'd be at my most powerful, simply because it was so obvious. So what was left?

Not much. My situation was really pretty desperate because I didn't have a thermal suit or even any breathing equipment. That limited me to planets which had low temperatures and atmospheres with lots of oxygen. Prxtln was cold enough, only I couldn't breathe there. On Mbridlengile, I would be not only too hot and unable to breathe, but also a victim of the carnivorous lichen. Was pitifully obvious Ja-Ja-Bee my only choice?

It was, I decided. Then I lost the roll for planet envelopes, giving me last choice. Zena got to pick first. With a big grin in my direction, she drew Ja-Ja-Bee.

I was baffled. Ja-Ja-Bee was useless to her—unless she knew I had The Piggy. But how could she know?

I picked Prxtln, hopelessly, and then two other planets, without thinking much about it. One of them was all blazing desert, a furnace as far as Luap was concerned. The other was a yellowish planet named Teon with a nice oxygen atmosphere, but still far too warm. Where was I going to hide The Piggy?

Now the others were busily stuffing their envelopes. The Piggy grinned vacantly at me from my hand, as simple and artless as a child's drawing. And it still gave me a jolt to look at it, the feeling of something jumping out at me in the dark.

"We're waiting, Barney," Zena said.

The others had finished with their envelopes and were complacently sipping wine. They were smiling at me, apparently friendly: Zena, Manny, and Joe, the glamorous people next door, who really did seem to like me after all, forgiving me for this afternoon, including me in their game.

Only right now, they were a hairy spider-lady; a fish-man with a long, razor-sharp horn growing out of his head; and a flying octopus with claws. And they would happily kill me to get the smiling pink thing in my hand.

I looked quickly away from the gruesome trio and back to my hand. And I noticed something I had missed before: Teon had two little ice caps on its poles, like Earth. Glacial

91

areas where I could breathe and also be comfortable. Suddenly I became very busy with my cards.

"Ready," I said. Joe pressed the timer, and the game was on.

The game went fast with four players, especially since all the others seemed to have their strategies well planned, moving purposefully across the board. My only strategy was not to make it obvious that I had hidden anything important on Teon, which happened to be the closest planet to my starting point of Ja-Ja-Bee. I left home and moved as quickly as possible in the opposite direction from Teon, hoping to lead them off the track.

Then Zulma landed on a blinking star, and took an instruction card which ordered her to land directly on the surface of Ja-Ja-Bee, where she was to spend her next three turns.

"Poor fat Zulma," Moyna giggled. "Your bloated brain won't save you now."

I understood Moyna's glee at getting the dangerous intelligent spider-lady so quickly out of the game. Would the atmosphere poison her before she had time to freeze to death? I was curious to see.

But Zulma wasn't perturbed. She had brought portable breathing equipment with her. And, since Ja-Ja-Bee had been one of the planets she had chosen at the beginning, she had stashed a powerful heat pump there, as well as a cache of freeze-dried mosquito larvae, her favorite food. She had a nice, cozy little sojourn, saving up fuel, biding her time—and she was now conveniently close to Teon, which made me uneasy.

My uneasiness grew when I noticed that Moyna and Jrlb were both zeroing in on Teon as well. My long brooding over the cards, added to the fact that Teon was the only planet I had chosen on which I could survive, must have tipped all three of them off. They all knew The Piggy was on Teon—and meanwhile, I had stupidly put myself halfway across the universe from it.

On my next turn I reversed direction and began heading back. It was sadly obvious, but what else could I do?

When Zulma's waiting period was up, she rolled a 9, which brought her only three stars from Teon. In another move, she'd be there.

Then Jrlb took his turn, and landed on the same star as Zulma. That meant direct combat in space.

The game was so hypnotic that I could almost see Zulma strapping on her breathing gear and scrabbling out of the ammonia lock. In my imagination—aided by the rule book—her abdomen throbbed, spinnerets wriggled. Sticky threads emerged, attaching themselves to her ship's hull. Zulma launched herself into space, propelling herself by spewing out thread behind her, which had the strength of coaxial cable and kept her safely anchored to her ship.

Water-breathing Jrlb also had portable breathing equipment. Even so, on the surface of most planets he would have been at a terrible disadvantage, since the water in his tanks weighed a ton per cubic meter on Earth. But he was in space now, so the tanks weighed nothing. He also had a mini-rocket strapped between his legs, which enabled him to propel himself in any direction. In combination with his sleek swimmer's body it made him spectacularly agile. He zoomed from his ship, his sword pointed directly at Zulma's soft underbelly.

Zulma could move by spewing out thread, but she couldn't retract it. Smart as she was, in space she was infinitely slower and clumsier than Jrlb.

Jrlb darted ahead of Zulma and sliced her cable in two with his sword. Zulma rolled and tumbled helplessly, tangled in cord, separated from her ship. Jrlb dived and then came up from below her, his sword slashing through the vacuum. A couple of strokes, and the cord wrapped around her would be in shreds, and after that, her abdomen.

"Go get her, Jrlb! Slice her to ribbons!" urged the fragile, delicate Moyna in Manny's breathy squeal. I was actually beginning to feel sorry for Zulma, so awkward and helpless.

But I had forgotten about her brain. Zulma wouldn't have left her ship without another card up her sleeve. It was a laser gun, clutched in her maw. As Jrlb came up from below for the kill, she let him have it.

It was all over in a flash; he didn't even have a chance to utter his death bellow. Quietly his tanks dissolved; there would only be the hiss of water vaporizing. Nothing was left of him but the charred, twisted remains of his once mighty sword, spinning away, I imagined, to drift eternally in space.

"Three-man game," Joe grunted, slamming down his hand.

"Too bad, Joe," said Zena matter-of-factly, grabbing his cards without looking up. Zulma busily went through the attributes she had won from Jrlb, to see if there were any worth keeping.

That reminded me that there were other attribute cards stashed away on various planets. I was quite close to Flaeioub, which, I remembered, was one of Moyna's envelopes. I could breathe on Flaeioub. I took the risk of darting down there on my next turn, instead of continuing

94

to head back to Teon. And I was in luck. Moyna had left the Portable Access to Hyperspace card in her envelope. There was only one of them in the whole deck, and it functioned exactly like the black funnels on the board: It took you anywhere instantly.

But why would Moyna leave such an important card at home? She wasn't stupid—her IRSC number was better than my character's. I hadn't read all of the rule book, but I had made a special point of looking up the IRSC. The higher—or worse—a character's number was, the fewer clever moves he was allowed to make, because he wouldn't be smart enough to think of them. The lower his number was, the more moves were available. And so I was a little shocked, as well as elated, that Moyna would leave the hyperspace card behind.

In my excitement, it didn't occur to me that Moyna must have had a reason for doing it—such as wanting to keep an even more powerful card in her hand. . . .

I took the hyperspace card, leaving one of my own in its place, as the rules stated. I entered hyperspace and was instantly on the northern ice cap of Teon, guarding The Piggy, ahead of the other two.

Moyna moved six stars closer. Then Zulma hit another instruction card: You, and the closest player in transit, proceed to surface of nearest planet for mutually beneficial trade.

Only, with me already there, it wouldn't be "mutually beneficial trade." It would be combat, two against one.

It was late autumn on Teon, according to the timetable in the rule book, and the northern polar cap would be entering into its winter of perpetual night. I stood on an ice field. A shriveled corona of dusk lay weakly on the horizon. As I pictured the scene, vast onrushing shadows of distant cliffs, magnified out of all proportion by the departing sun, swept over and swallowed the last raised patches of dully glittering snow around me.

Only two shapes were high enough still to be touched by a dying orange glow as they swooped toward me. I imagined Moyna's head billowing in the rush of her descent, her tentacles undulating behind her, each ending in a vulture's claw. Zulma would be a fat blemish on the sky, black as the speeding cliff shadows, except for the last of the sunlight that twinkled and flashed from her needlelike teeth and many faceted eyes.

And they were chatting quite amiably, out of earshot, trading attributes, making deals—all aimed at getting rid of me.

I began to panic. My lighting equipment would have been an advantage, only I had exchanged it for Moyna's hyperspace card. I had a disguise card, enabling me to resemble the inhabitants of the planet, but no locals lived up here—my pursuers would know it was me, no matter what I looked like. I had some kind of neural whip, but that wouldn't be much help against Zulma's laser gun—especially since she'd be able to see much better than me, with her enormous eyes. I had something called euphoric gas, but I hadn't had a chance to find out what that would do to them—or to me. I had plenty of food and water, and I had the built-in bodily advantage of being comfortable at this temperature. But with *their* lethal bodily advantages, they could dispense with me so fast they'd be out of here before they had time to feel the slightest chill—even without Zulma's heat pump.

The last threadlike glow shrank beneath the horizon. My pursuers grew rapidly larger and less distinct in the enveloping dimness.

But I had forgotten something: the slug that lived in my mouth. The slug was a brain without a body, who could not move or see or touch or smell on his own, but who could survive by absorbing the remnants of food left on my teeth. And who, when agreeably satiated, would repay me by improving my IRSC to an absolutely transcendent 3.9.

"Are you ever going to wake up and eat something, you cretin?" he reminded me. I was so caught up in the game, I could almost hear his voice, a petulant sour twang. It was his hungry voice, and it wasn't pleasant. "Spider meat," he suggested. "I'm in the mood for some nice crunchy little spiders."

Reptile though I was, spiders were my least favorite food—and hairy Zulma bearing down on me didn't make the thought any more appetizing. Still, I had a good supply of them. I shoved several handfuls into my mouth, frantically gobbling them down.

"Hey, slow it down, you retard!" the slug peeped piercingly at me, curled up against my palate out of danger from my teeth. "I've told you over and over again! You must masticate your food *properly*. Otherwise it does me no good at all."

Slowly, thoroughly, I chewed. In the imaginary gloom, Zulma seemed to have landed about a hundred yards away from me. Moyna was a pale shape beside her. The low hydrogen here had been the cause of Moyna's rapid descent, and now she seemed to be able to hover only inches above the ice, moving slowly. As my slug grew full, my IRSC began moving toward 10, and I began speculating about Moyna's trump card—the card so powerful she had left her hyperspace card at home for me to take. There weren't many cards that powerful.

"Ah, that's a little better now," chirped my slug, whose name was Zshoozsh, a little more amiably. "I feel just energetic enough to start tossing you some really scintillating hormones, pal." He went into meditation. My IRSC zoomed past 7, past 5, all the way to 3.9.

Of course, Zshoozsh wasn't trying to save my hide purely out of the goodness of his nonexistent heart. He simply knew that if I went, he went too.

If Luap's IRSC had been this low from the beginning, of course, he would have had more options. He would have taken The Piggy immediately from Teon and zipped home with the hyperspace card. Luap at IRSC 25, however, had not been allowed by the rules to make that move. He had stood and watched the eerie sunset and fretted. And now, since the others had landed, direct combat could not be avoided.

But Luap at 3.9 might be brilliant enough to make up for his near fatal blunder. Moyna, sagging and limp as a deflated inner tube, was too sluggish and earthbound to be much of a threat. Zulma, with her heat pump and breathing gear, was the real danger. And she knew it too. I couldn't see much, but I was intelligent enough to interpret the most minimal signals. Zulma was taking aim with the laser gun.

I lashed out with the neural whip, sending the laser gun spinning off into the distance and stunning Zulma briefly. But only briefly. In the next instant she was upon me, knocking me to the ice with her superior weight, slashing with her pincers. I couldn't slide out from under her. The bottom half of her face fell open. Paralyzing fangs lunged for my neck.

I popped the capsule of euphoric gas. It was a risk, because I did not have the antidote. But it was my only chance. And perhaps my superior intellect would leave me less incapacitated than her.

We rolled away from each other, giggling. Zulma lay helplessly on her back, flailing her legs and gasping out nasty spider limericks in her native tongue. I was smart enough to understand them. In any other condition they would have repelled me, but in my drunken state I thought they were hilarious. I lay there and laughed at her wit, and thought about how beautiful the black ice field looked against the almost as black sky.

My super intelligence did tell me what card Moyna must have, as she dragged herself, her limbs nearly inflexible with cold, to The Piggy. But I didn't bother trying to stop her. "Oh, Zulma, I can't *stand* it!" I wailed in mirth. "The irony's too much. Poor dumb little Moyna, and all the time she had the Portable Access to the Fifth-Dimensional Matrix." I emitted another shriek. "And now she has the hyperspace card back too!"

Then Moyna was gone. Zulma and I both felt it. Just as the hyperspace card took you out of normal space, so that you could go anywhere in an instant, the fifth-dimensional matrix card took you out of time. Moyna, with The Piggy in tow, could now go any*when* she would like. And naturally she took The Piggy to the end of the game, when the alarm went off.

Luap and Zulma were still trapped in real time. And The Piggy was eternally out of reach to them. They could do nothing but wait until the end of the game, anticipating the loss of their lives and their planets.

Fortunately, since there hadn't been much time left in the game anyway, their gassed euphoria persisted until it was over, preventing them from suffering as much as they might have.

But as soon as the alarm went, the euphoria went too. The three losing planets blinked off the board.

"What a loathsome sound that thing makes!" Zena said, quickly switching it off.

"It sounds quite cheerful and mellifluous to me," Manny said, displaying the round smirking Piggy to all of us.

"Watch it, Manny," Zena warned him. There was no humor in her voice; she was a poor loser. "Don't shove it. You cheated back there. You didn't inform me you had the fifth-dimensional matrix. Things might have been otherwise if you had."

"You didn't ask me," Manny pointed out. "I didn't cheat at all. And anyway, you were planning to kill me down on that ice cap, as soon as you got rid of Lu—Barney, weren't you."

"I don't want to talk about it!" She pushed her chair back and stood up from the table. She stared down at me. "I don't like it when people keep things hidden from me," she said, quite slowly. "It makes me very mean."

She stared at me for so long it began to seem a little strange. "What are you looking at *me* for? I didn't hide anything from you," I said, quite truthfully—I was still too caught up in the game to remember what was going on outside the game. "We both lost. Fair and square."

Now Joe was watching me too, chewing grimly at his

lip, but I still couldn't figure out what might be the matter with them. The game had left me in a kind of stupefied daze. It was more intense than the way I felt after finishing an exciting book. It had been like actually *being* in the book. Was Joe angry because I had lasted longer than he had?

"I think Barney played very decently for a beginner," Manny said, with a nervous little smile. Their unsportsmanlike behavior was taking away his pleasure in winning. "He'll be a real whiz after a few more games."

"*If* we ever let him play again," Zena said. She had become another person, some kind of cold evil queen out of a fairy tale. "We don't like playing with liars and cheats."

Then Joe's mood sudddenly shifted. "Oh, relent, Zena. You know we must play with him again. It's the only . . . It's not right to get someone involved and then suddenly exclude them. And you have to confess, Barney has talent. He almost came close to winning, on his first four-man game—if Manny hadn't had the fifth-dimensional matrix. That card's hard to beat."

"The fifth-dimensional matrix didn't help Luap very much," Manny said, with a surprisingly bitter laugh. "That's what got us into this whole mess. If it weren't for that we'd—"

"For God's sake, Manny!" Zena cried, swiftly turning away from me, her voice shrill.

Manny didn't know where to look, or what to say. He seemed terribly embarrassed. If he hadn't been so tanned, he might have been blushing.

"Huh?" I said, confused. "But I . . . Luap *didn't* have the fifth-dimensional matrix. You did, Moyna—I mean

101

Manny. What are you all...?" I sank into my chair, shaking my head.

"Manny was just referring to a game we played the other day," Joe explained.

"Oh. I see," I said. But why should that account for Zena's horrified response and Manny's shamed reactions? They had been so friendly before the game; now that it was over, nothing they did was making any sense. I looked at my watch. It was a quarter to ten. Gratefully, I stood up.

"I guess it's time for me to go now," I said. "Anyway, I don't want to intrude. Thanks for letting me play. It was wonderful. I really would like to play again." I was backing for the door.

"Of course you can," Manny assured me.

"You'll *have* to play again," Joe said, with a kind of forced heartiness. "You're part of it now."

Zena watched me silently as I left.

Mom and Dad—or, as I was beginning to think of them, the *new* Mom and Dad—once again plied me with questions about the neighbors. They behaved as though I had just spent the evening with celebrities. Mom, who was still rather envious, refused to believe at first that we had done nothing but play an imaginary space game. She childishly accused me of hiding something, until it became obvious, when I began to describe the game, that I was telling the truth. "Well, it certainly is very generous of them to stoop to entertaining you with that kind of kid stuff," she said. "But don't expect it to go on. By now, they must be dying for some mature, sophisticated company, I would think."

I got away from them as soon as I could. In my bedroom, my wet jeans, still draped over the chair, had made a blue puddle on the floor.

Then I remembered the little box in the drawer—the box the neighbors were looking for.

I had just assumed that when they didn't find it, they would think someone else had found it years ago. At least I hoped that's what they would think. They wouldn't suspect naive innocent little Barney.

Or would they?

Was *that* why Zena had called me a liar and a cheat? How suspicious of me were they? Then I thought of how I still had the document, and felt cold all over. As soon as they noticed it was missing—if they hadn't noticed already—they would *know* I had found the box. Zena had said she could be very mean when people hid things from her. I believed her.

I put on a pair of cotton pajamas, closed the door of my room, and took the box out of the drawer. I sat down on the bed and looked at it carefully for the first time. It was, as it had originally appeared, a tarnished black metal box. But now I saw that it was a box with a hinge, and a lid, and a simple latch that held the lid in place. It opened easily.

The bundle inside was wrapped in old, yellowed pages from some book—the few legible remnants of archaic type were proof of their age. The only reason there was any paper left at all was that it had been protected by the box and the trunk and the boards on top of them. There was nothing as convenient as a date on the pages, but they did seem to indicate that the bundle had not been disturbed for quite some time.

I tried to unwrap the papers carefully, but they disintegrated at the lightest touch. And my hands, shaking with excitement, were clumsier than usual. Was it possible that this actually *was* the trinket the captain had mentioned, the ornament his brother had taken from the murdered sailor? And that perhaps, when they got home, the captain had hidden it in the trunk on the island? Was I the first person who had touched it since then?

There was no hope of preserving the old papers. I tore them away and lifted out what was inside.

It was a small round object that fit easily in my hand, lightweight. Its surface had not cracked or split with age, nor had the paint faded. It was a garish pink, as flawless and glossy and smooth as if it had been painted yesterday. My excitement drained away. This couldn't be the old trinket after all, despite its wrappings. It was obviously too new. Disappointed, I turned it over. Then I cried out.

There was a face carved on this side, nothing but a rigid, slightly smiling mouth under a single wide-open eye. The lips and eye were sculpted in sharp relief. The vertical iris, inlaid in bright silver, gave the eye a piercing alertness. Crude as it was, the thing seemed alive. And it was the brutal wrongness of it, the mouth smiling with such placid idiocy, noseless, under the solitary gaping eye, that made the face so repellent.

The Piggy.

10

But it couldn't be the *real* Piggy.

The silver eye stared into mine with keen perception; the lilting mouth seemed to be trying not to laugh.

Just in time I heard footsteps and slithered under the sheet with my findings. The door creaked open. It was only Mom.

"Barney, I thought I heard you. . . .You're as white as a sheet! What's the matter?"

My face was too burned to be white, but I could feel that the blood had drained from it. "Nothing. I just came to an exciting place in my book," I said. Luckily, there was a paperback opened on the bed.

"Well, you've had an exhausting day and I don't want you staying up late reading. I'll be back in ten minutes to make sure your light's out." She started to leave, then turned back. "And I think you'd better take it easy tomorrow. You've been overtaxing yourself."

"Okay," I agreed, picking up the book.

As soon as she left, I pulled The Piggy out from under the sheet. The interruption had brought me back to the real world; I could look at the face now without feeling crazy. It was the unexpectedness of finding it, so soon after playing the game, that had given me such a jolt.

It was just a missing piece from a board game, that was all. There was nothing sinister about that. A little toy sculpture of The Piggy card. Naturally the neighbors, addicts of the game that they were, would be eager to get it back. The game wouldn't be right without it. You couldn't play Scrabble correctly without all the tiles.

But how often did you search out a missing Scrabble tile by finding it mentioned in a hundred-year-old document? A document that directed you to a place you had never been before? A piece of a futuristic science fiction game, not even on the market yet, "misplaced" where it had not been disturbed for decades.

The intelligent deformed eye knew exactly what I was thinking; the leering mouth mocked me. I covered it with my hand.

My next impulse was to run right over and give it to them. "Here, take it, it's yours, I don't want anything to do with it," I would say, thrusting it at them. And be rid of the pink and foul and mischievous thing, with all its impossible connotations.

Then I could stop worrying about it, because of course they would leave, immediately. This was what they had come here to find. And once they had it, they wouldn't tell me the truth about what it was, or how the whole puzzle fit together. They wanted to keep their true purpose a secret. Otherwise they could have simply asked me if I'd found anything like The Piggy at the very beginning.

But they hadn't. They had searched the entire house, cleverly sidestepping all of my questions. They had avoided telling me anything about why they were really here, including me only as a fourth player in a make-believe game. And if I gave them what they wanted now, I would never find out anything else.

I gritted my teeth, unfolded my hand, and stared down at The Piggy again. It was repulsive, all right, but that was the least important thing about it. What was I so afraid of, anyway? What was it going to do to me? Why give it up now? It was ugly, but it was *good*—it was what everyone wanted. It was the prize.

And now I had it, and they didn't.

Suddenly I felt like Luap as his IRSC zoomed to 3.9. And I only had a minute to look at the document before Mom came back to check that the light was out. I got it from the drawer and hastily reread the relevant parts. "A trinket" was all the captain had said about the object his brother had found. About the "sailor" he had taken it from, he was more specific: "greenish, *reptilian* hide"; "some *invertebrate* organism, gelatinous, sluglike, protruding from the cracked, blackened lips"; "the *third* eye."

This was not the only place I had run across that description. Luap!

I put The Piggy and the document under my pillow and turned out the light.

The captain had believed he was describing a hallucination. But his description of the murdered sailor, who had been carrying the trinket, tallied precisely with the character Luap in the game. And then I remembered Manny saying, just a little while ago, "The fifth-dimensional matrix didn't help Luap very much. That's what got us into this whole mess. . . ."

Then Zena had shrilled at him to shut up. And Manny had seemed horrified at his blunder. And I had been confused, because Manny's remark hadn't made sense in the context of the game we had played. "A game we played the other day," Joe had explained.

A real game, perhaps? Like the board game, but with a real Piggy, and real space travelers? A game in which the not very bright Luap had used the fifth-dimensional matrix to travel back to 1864—and then lost The Piggy when his blood boiled in the South Pacific climate?

I *felt* as though I were being rational now. But I had come back to the same insane idea that had hit me when I first saw The Piggy. It was impossible, it was totally fantastic. And yet I could come up with no other explanation that made sense of everything, that was so simple and direct.

I made an agreement with myself to think of it as merely a hypothesis—that was the rational thing to do. Then I lay there in the dark, alert, growing more and more excited. And more impressed with myself. If the game *was* real, then, ignorant though I had been, I had still done exactly what I should have done in order to win. I had managed to get my hands on The Piggy. How could I have considered running over there like a baby and handing it back to them? It looked horrible, but what it really meant was safety. And now I had it under my pillow.

Then my thoughts swerved again, and I had the sensation of a hand drifting along my spine in the darkness. Yes, The Piggy meant safety—but *only at the end* of the game. The rest of the time, The Piggy meant danger. The Piggy was what all the players wanted. "You will stop at *nothing* to gain possession of it," I heard Zena saying, yesterday, on the sunny patio.

It wasn't sunny now. I lay there and listened to the gravelly wet rumble of the surf, to the wind breathing in the marsh grasses. There were no sounds of automobiles or radios, only the mindless screaming gulls. Outside, the night would be broken only by a few distant, unreachable pinpoints of light.

Unless, of course, the neighbors were still awake in their pink cottage, the picture window casting its pale distorted oblong across the lawn. I thought of the last gray patches of daylight on the ice cap of Teon and the cliff shadows sweeping over them. I felt as isolated as Luap standing there. The neighbors' cottage was so very close—closer even than Zulma and Moyna hurtling out of the sky, swooping quickly down for The Piggy.

"It's only a hypothesis, you jerk," I whispered to myself, huddled under the sheet, my head pressed against the pillow. The pillow was thin, the objects underneath it lumpy. But where else could I put them? Where else would they be safe when Zena, or Manny, or Joe, or all three, came creeping in?

Zena and Manny and Joe, who made a different impression on everyone. I remembered the disguise card I hadn't used, the card that gave the player the ability to resemble the inhabitants of a foreign planet. Did the neighbors have such equipment? And if so, what did they really look like? Was that rustling noise the curtain, or was it Moyna floating in the window? Was it one of her talons that seemed to be hovering just above my neck?

But Moyna couldn't exist. She was as biologically hopeless as the slugs in the book I had been reading, nothing but a character in a game. Zulma and Jrlb didn't rent cinder-block cottages on the beach, or eat bagels and cream cheese for breakfast. And there was no planet called Earth in the game, and no human characters—no Barney, no Mom and Dad.

It was childish of me, but the thought of the two of them in the next room did give me a certain comfort. Mom and Dad were too ordinary, even dull, to exist in a universe in which Interstellar Pig was possible. And anyway, they wouldn't let anything happen to me; they were both light sleepers.

If they were still asleep, that is, and not dead. Moyna could move very quietly. And lethal bacteria were quieter still. Maybe it would be a good idea to get up and check on them, just to make sure they were still breathing.

But if I did that, it would be as good as admitting that I really did have something to be afraid of. There had to be some other explanation for The Piggy and the captain and all the rest. In a minute it would come to me; then I would be able to relax and go to sleep.

But it didn't come. And the effort to find it only kept me wide awake. After a while, I could no longer prevent myself from looking at the bedside clock. It was 3 A.M. That was depressing. On the other hand, if the neighbors really were going to attack, wouldn't they have done it by now? Why should they wait? They were probably just asleep. And I could find out easily enough by looking out the window, to see if their lights were out. Then I'd be able to stop torturing myself.

I got up and tiptoed to the window and looked out. I groaned quietly and covered my eyes with my hand. All the lights in the cottage were on. Now I was beginning to feel angry. Why couldn't they just go to bed at a reasonable time like everyone else, instead of staying awake and making me worry?

But maybe they had just forgotten to turn the lights out. I looked again. I couldn't see inside. There was a kind of shadow in the patch of light on the front lawn. Probably that maroon plastic chair—it was squat and lumpy enough.

Then the shadow waddled, bulbous and spiderlike; something thin and segmented quivered beside it, as though it was gesturing with one of its legs.

I was back under the sheet, clutching the pillow. Mom and Dad, Mom and Dad in the next room, I kept reminding myself, meanwhile imagining the creatures next door planning their strategy. The attack would have to be soon, while it was still dark, and Zulma's eyes would give her an advantage. I should be back at the window, prepared to defend The Piggy. More nervous than ever now, I listened for the sounds of scrabbling feet, for the rhythmic hiss of breathing gear.

The next time I opened my eyes, gray light was coming through the window. The sun was rising. I got up again. And now the cottage windows were dark.

Then I did sleep fitfully for a few hours. It was midmorning when I awoke. Sunlight beat against the windows, the room was stifling and I was drenched in sweat. I didn't feel rested at all, my sunburn hurt worse than ever, and now, in addition, all my muscles were sore from yesterday's exertions on the island.

But in the sunlight I was able to look back on my fears

in the darkness as imaginary, the result of the neighbors' addictive, hallucinatory game. I vowed not to indulge in the game for another day or two, at least. Today I would take advantage of my condition and play the invalid. I would stay at home, avoid the neighbors while I sorted things out, and let Mom feed me and take care of me.

I yawned, and then climbed out of bed as delicately as an old man with arthritis. I limped around, getting out of my pajamas and into a pair of shorts. Mom must have heard my footsteps, because a moment later she knocked at the door. "Can I come in, Barney?" she said.

"Sure." I arranged myself back on the bed, trying to look weak.

I had never been happier to see Mom's ordinary, homely face as she came into the room. Only now she seemed so girlishly excited that she was hardly homely at all. She wore a new outfit, white shorts and a middy blouse, and she had tied a bright silk scarf around her head. Her skin was finally beginning to look tanned instead of pink—the color gave a youthful quality to her middle-aged features. "I was hoping you'd get up soon," she said. "I didn't want to wake you, you seemed so exhausted last night. How do you feel?"

"Not so great," I said, feeble but brave. "I think maybe I should take it easy, maybe just stay around the house—"

"I think that's just exactly what you need," she burst in, hardly giving me a chance to finish. "There's some granola, and some sandwiches in the fridge for later, so you should be fine until we get back. And *please* don't go out in the sun."

I sat up quickly on the bed. "Get back? From where?"

"Oh, those marvelous friends next door, they're so thoughtful!" she gushed. "They had plans to go sailing with the Powells today, but now two of them can't go—some kind of business calls they have to wait for. So one of the men—Joe, the big handsome one—invited your father and me to go instead. With the Powells, can you imagine? All my friends will die!"

"The Powells?" I said. "Who are they?"

"Only one of the oldest families on this part of the coast." Mom looked in the mirror over the dresser and adjusted her scarf. "They're supposed to have the most fabulous summer house. You have to summer here for years before getting an invitation from them. And Joe says we'll be sailing way out in the ocean, not the bay." She sounded like a fourteen-year-old.

"But wait a minute," I said. "Don't you think ... I mean, are you sure ... I mean, out on the ocean, if a storm comes up, will you be safe?"

She laughed. "Barney, it's the most gorgeous day we've had yet. Now you take care of yourself. I've kept Joe waiting long enough, waiting for you to wake up."

"But ... but what about ..." I couldn't think of anything to say, except that I didn't think they'd be safe with Joe, and I didn't want to be left alone. But I couldn't say that.

"We'll be back before dark, Barney. Have a restful day," she cried gaily, and left.

I sank back onto the bed, feeling more tired than ever. The pattern of yesterday's game seemed to be repeating itself: Joe out of the way, but Zena and Manny—or was it Zulma and Moyna—to contend with. In my exhausted state, one of them would have been more than enough.

And how soon would it be before they came swooping down?

I turned over and tried to go back to sleep.

11

I was awakened by a crash downstairs.

I lay there, my heart pounding. There were no footsteps or voices. Despite the crash, the house was empty.

But not quiet. The windowpanes rattled in my room, the kitchen screen door was banging, the thudding of the surf sounded as close as the front porch. And it was strangely dark outside, though the clock told me it was not quite 6 P.M.

I raced to the window. The sky boiled with thick purple clouds, the usually placid bay seethed with foam. Beside the marsh, the stunted scrub pines were bent over and trembling. And the Volkswagen—with Joe and Mom and Dad—had not returned.

I raced around the house, shutting windows against the first raindrops. I picked up the living room lamp that had awakened me when it had been toppled by a gust of wind. Then I struggled to find a station on the radio that was not obliterated by static, listening continually for the Volkswagen. Finally I managed to find a crackling voice bleating something about small craft warnings. It was lucky the storm had come so late in the day. They would have been back on shore before it got rough. They were probably on their way home this very minute.

I hadn't been asleep all day. I had spent a lot of time in bed at first, waiting for Zena and Manny to show up, getting up frequently to look at them from the window. They were lying in their bikinis on the patio in front of their house, reading, occasionally eating. They were staying close to home to make sure I wouldn't get away—and at any moment they could come to get me.

It got too nerve-racking to lie there and wait for them, so I began trying to find a good hiding place for The Piggy. I did a long, thorough job, checking out every room in the house, using the flashlight to explore dark corners. I finally ended up in the living room. There were built-in bookcases on either side of the fireplace, crammed with books all the way from the floor to the ceiling. The books were so dusty that it seemed no one had even pulled one off the shelf for years. They all looked so boring and dated they would probably stay there untouched until they rotted. And I remembered a story I'd read about jewel smugglers. . . .

I climbed up on a chair. Very carefully, so as not to disturb the dust, I pulled out the most inaccessible volume from the righthand corner of the topmost shelf, where the brick chimney met the beamed ceiling. It turned out to be a yearbook from some local high school, class of 1950. It was not the kind of thing the neighbors would be interested in, even if they happened to notice it; and they'd never notice it because it was too high up, several feet above even Zena's eye level. With a kitchen shears I slashed a hole through the senior class photos, the girls with their sweaters and pearls and funny permed hair, the boys with crew cuts and bow ties, all of them with quotes under their pictures like Still Waters Run Deep (she must have been a shy, unpopular one), or We Are All in the Gutter, but Some of Us Are Looking at the Stars (that quote elicited more interesting speculations). The hole was just over half an inch thick, from Linda Finkel to Polly Winters.

The Piggy fit easily inside. Since the hole was only a couple of inches square, in the middle of the pages, the book looked perfectly ordinary when closed. I replaced it on the shelf. Then, using Mom's makeup brush and cotton puff, I rearranged the dust on the shelf so carefully that even Sherlock Holmes wouldn't have suspected the book had been touched for decades.

The Piggy was safe now. And what was most brilliant about the hiding place was how brazen it was, right out in the open in the living room, where no one would ever think of looking, instead of in some dark obvious hole in the basement or up above the rafters. Let them find another excuse for searching the house, let them poke around wherever they wanted. They'd never get their hands on it now without information from me. And that would not be forthcoming until I received the information I wanted from them.

After all, if it *was* the real Piggy, and the game *was* real, then finding a good hiding place for it was only what I was expected to do, perfectly fair, according to the rules. . . .

"But it's not real," I assured myself. I was beginning to lose track of how much I was talking to myself. I kept picking up books and throwing them down, pacing around the house as the afternoon dragged endlessly on, waiting for the Volkswagen to return. Every once in a while, I peeked out at Zena and Manny, still sunbathing on the patio.

A nap would be a good way of killing time until Mom and Dad came back. I lay down on my bed on top of the sheet, aware that The Piggy was nowhere near me, edgy about Mom and Dad. But I was also tired enough to fall asleep.

Until the sounds of the storm woke me up. After hearing the news about small craft warnings on the radio, I began to get really worried. Obviously Joe had taken them sailing to get them out of the way. They would have interfered with the attack on me. And when was it going to come?

And then I did hear the labored grunt of the Volkswagen motor ascending the hill, and the crunch of tires on gravel. What a baby I was to get myself so worked up! Mom and Dad were adults. They knew how to take care of themselves. I stepped out onto the front porch.

Zena and Manny, fully clothed now, were coming from the cottage to greet Joe. The roof of the convertible had been put up against the impending rain. The motor died. Joe stepped out of the driver's seat, his hair lifted by the wind.

It was too overcast for any kind of sunset. Behind the pink cottage, over the dark water, there was only the thinnest line of orange, shrinking quickly behind the clouds.

I waited. Joe locked his door, then went around to the other side of the car. He made sure that door was locked, and the window rolled up. The few fat raindrops didn't seem to be bothering him as he slowly walked toward Zena and Manny, standing stiffly by their front door.

There was no one else in the car.

I didn't think. I ran. They didn't see me, turned away to
enter their cottage. I grabbed Joe's elbow and spun him
around. "Where are they?" I screamed.

Joe seemed startled, but his grin was easy and benign.
"Didn't they call you yet?" he asked me.

"What do you mean, call me? Where are they?"

Joe laughed, then turned to glance at Zena and Manny,
who were smiling. "Barney, what a state you're in!" Joe
said. "It's not the end of the world. Your parents—who
were quite amusing, by the way—" he put in to the others,
"hit it off splendidly with the Powells, who invited them
to have dinner at their house."

"I don't believe it," I said. "I don't believe you even
know those people."

Joe rolled his eyes. "You're being silly, Barney. Anyway, they're going to call you. I'm surprised they haven't done it by now. It was a good half hour ago."

"You don't have the number where I can call them?"

Zena giggled. "Do they still give you numbers to call every time they go out to dinner, Barney, at your age? Or maybe they usually hire a baby-sitter."

She had a point. Mom and Dad went out all the time at home without leaving me a way to reach them. Yet it seemed different this time. "No, they don't," I said, feeling foolish. "But you'd think they would have called me."

"Maybe you should check to see if the phone's working," Manny said, shivering. "This wind's pretty strong. A wire could have blown over somewhere. Maybe they did try to call and couldn't get through."

Joe was looking up at the sky, a calloused hand shielding his eyes from the thickening raindrops. "Looks like it's going to be a big storm," he observed.

"I'm going to check the phone," I said.

"Your mother asked if we would give you supper," Joe said, as I turned to get away from them. "I told her it would be our pleasure."

"Yes, Barney, you *must* have dinner with us!" Zena urged me, as hospitable as if the witch she had been last night had been a dream of mine. "Manny's a wonderful cook."

"We're having lobster," Manny called after me, as I reached the front steps. "And lime pie. You better hurry back. We're starving."

The phone in our kitchen, as Manny had suggested, was dead. I slammed it down, angry and bewildered and scared. Everything Joe said made sense; it was a perfectly reasonable thing for Mom and Dad to do. Only it was all

121

too conveniently neat. Last night the neighbors had suspected that I had The Piggy. Today, Joe takes Mom and Dad sailing. And then Mom and Dad *happen* to get invited to dinner, and then a storm *happens* to come up and the phone *happens* to go dead, so I can't check on it.

Did the neighbors have a storm-generating card among their attributes? And what was the next step in getting The Piggy—the step that made it necessary to get rid of Mom and Dad and the phone, so I would be alone and unable to call for help?

Maybe Joe had simply pushed them off the boat.

But I refused to believe they were dead. It was too dark in the kitchen now to see anything but the grayish light outside the windows. I twisted the switch on the nearest wall lamp, and the anchors and lighthouses on the shade winked on. At least the electricity was still working. Darkness didn't seem to be necessary for their plans.

I could always make the forty-five minute walk to the village, in the now heavily pelting rain. There might be a store open. Maybe even a police station, though I couldn't remember having noticed one. And what would I tell them, if I found one? The neighbors hadn't made any specific threats, hadn't done anything overt that anyone else would find suspicious. And of course they would cleverly deny it all. And everyone found them *so* likable. And they were adults and I was only a teenager. All I'd accomplish by going to town would be to make a fool of myself.

Or I could stay home alone and eat cold bologna instead of lobster. But that wouldn't keep them from coming over to get me—I'd just be missing a good meal, pointlessly. And they would tease me, and make me feel foolish for that.

I went upstairs and put on warmer clothes, listening to the rain as I changed. The sound reminded me to put on my slicker before I went out. I would have been drenched if I hadn't. As I ran across the dark lawn, I decided I had better keep an eye on Manny while he cooked. And I wouldn't take a bite of anything until I made sure the others had tasted it first.

"Isn't this quaint?" Zena greeted me. "Our first real storm. What is it they call them around here? Nor'easters, or something dramatic like that?"

There was a big roaring fire, and wonderful smells coming from the kitchen. Zena took my slicker like a gracious hostess. Was I sure I hadn't dreamed her behavior last night?

Manny was banging things around in the kitchen. Zena and Joe had drinks by the fire, and there was a plate of munchies—crackers and cheese and Zena's ubiquitous sliced onions. "Let me get you something to drink, Barney," Zena said.

"I can get it myself," I said. "I want to see what Manny's doing in there, that smells so good."

Manny bustled about among the clouds of steam like a frenzied alchemist in a knotty pine laboratory. He was in his element here, as he certainly hadn't been yesterday on the windsurfer. "Help yourself to any beverage you want, Barney; *we* won't let on to your parents," he said, conspiratorially. He told me where all the drink ingredients were, but I took only ginger ale from an unopened bottle—I wanted to keep my head clear. I asked him about what he was doing, and he eagerly explained, never stopping in his work as he babbled on about the best ways to cook string beans and new potatoes.

"Of course, some people claim you lose nutrients by using so much water, but they don't know what they're talking about. It's the great amount of water that makes them cook fast, so they're green and crisp. . . ."

I concentrated on checking the shelves and counters for any suspicious-looking substances, not paying much attention to what he was saying. "Uh-huh, that's interesting," I put in occasionally, noting the absence of rat poison, or any unlabeled containers.

". . . although drowning everything in butter can be fattening, and detrimental for the heart. But if you'd like to make a little *deal*, Barney, I could let you have some liquid that would keep your body, including all your organs, in perfect shape forever, no matter *what* you ate or drank. The others don't have anything like it."

"Uh-huh, anything like it, I see," I murmured, noticing how dusty the top of the refrigerator was. They weren't very good housekeepers.

"A youth serum is what you'd call it," he said, peering into the pot of lobsters. "You could have all the remainder of it, Barney. Of course, you wouldn't want to take it right away. Wait a few years, until you're in your early twenties, say. Then you'll just *stay* in your twenties, for good. Not to mention, it has the amusing little side effect of making you irresistibly attractive, along with the eternal youth part."

"Hmm, eternal youth," I said vaguely. "Sounds great. . . ." I took a sip of ginger ale. Then I almost dropped the glass. *"What?"* I said quite loudly, as his last few sentences finally sank in.

"Shhh!" Manny said, leaving his pots and pans now to pull me to the back door. We stepped just outside, under

124

the roof overhang, out of earshot of the others. "It's wonderful stuff, Barney, believe me, I wouldn't kid you," he said, nodding enthusiastically. I was near enough to him now to see that the close-cut hairs of his beard were as uniform and symmetrically spaced as nylon bristles on a mass-produced brush. "It may not be *literally* eternal, but it lasts quite long enough," Manny went on. "Look what it did to me. I'm 138—relatively speaking, of course. It's also fine for the complexion. Just give me The Piggy, Barney, and it's yours."

"The Piggy!" I cried out, overjoyed. I didn't know what this eternal youth bit was all about, but at that moment it didn't matter. What was so marvelous was that finally one of them was being honest with me about The Piggy. "The Piggy! That *is* what you want, right?" I demanded breathlessly. "That's why you came here? That's what's behind everything?"

"Of course," he said, a little impatiently. "So how about it? Is it a deal?"

"But how come all of a sudden you're admitting you want The Piggy?"

"*You* brought it to this point, Barney, not I," he said, looking hard at me. His childish enthusiasm was suddenly gone, his voice angrily petulant. "The beans are going to overcook if you keep me waiting any longer. The youth serum for The Piggy. Is it a deal or isn't it?"

My joy drained away. His "deal" was so insane that what he had said about The Piggy had lost its meaning. "I'm cold," I said, backing away. "I'm going to go sit by the fire."

"Don't forget my offer." He came toward me, the rubber spatula in his hand raised like a club. "And you will *not* divulge one word about it to the others," he hissed, so threateningly that all I could do was nod mutely, feeling like a dog about to be whipped.

"Oh, Barney, you've kept me *so* distracted my beans might have gone *limp*!" he cried out in his normal voice, for the others to hear. "Get back out in the living room and amuse Zena and Joe, you cute pest! They're not doing anything vital."

I scurried away, trying to act as if nothing had happened. But Zena giggled at me from her comfortable chair by the fire. "Don't worry about Manny, Barney," she said. "He imagines it's the end of the world if the string beans aren't *al dente*." She nodded at the pink wicker love seat facing the fireplace. "Sit down. Relax."

I lowered myself onto the uncomfortable wicker. "Where's Joe?" I asked her.

"Removing his sheets and blankets from the clothesline. The dope hung them up to air out this morning and forgot all about them." She leaned toward me intimately. "Poor, absentminded Joe. He never contrived to get his hands on any intelligence booster." She paused, letting the words hang invitingly between us. "It's rare stuff, Barney. Very rare indeed. I won't inform you what I had to go through to get *my* hands on it." She put her hand on my knee. "But I'll give it to you, Barney. All you have to do is let me have The Piggy. Okay?"

Now she was doing it too. It was unnerving, but I wasn't as unprepared as I had been with Manny. "So you admit The Piggy's what you're after?" I asked. "You've been looking for a long time. And you found the document, and that's how you knew it was here, right?" She nodded. "But *why*? What does it really do? And why didn't you just—"

"Yes, that was very clever of you, stealing the document," she interrupted me, barely whispering. Her enchanting smile was so close to my face that she could have kissed me. "But you weren't clever enough to do it undetected, were you? Or to prevent us from discovering that you had The Piggy? You weren't clever enough for many things. *But you would be.*" Not taking her eyes from my face, she moved to the love seat and sat close beside me. "Only a milligram halves your IRSC; two milligrams quarter it. You'd be the genius of your age, Barney, of your entire *race*. The greatest works of art, the world-shaking inventions would all come from you. And that wouldn't mean only wealth and fame, Barney. Think about it. It would mean *power*." She gripped both my hands. "You'd be the most important person on this planet. Inevitably. All you have to do is to give me that superfluous little trinket. Just say yes, Barney."

I knew there was a flaw in what she was saying, aside from the unreality of any "intelligence booster." But her closeness made me a little dizzy. I closed my eyes. What was the flaw? And my brain, feeble and unboosted though it was, came up with the right answer. "But why do *you* want The Piggy, then, if it's just a superfluous little trinket like you say?" I asked her. "What *exactly* does it do?"

I opened my eyes. She was smiling, but it was fixed, an effort. "There's no time for all that now," she said, her whisper growing urgent. "With the brain booster, you'll understand everything anyway. It's more precious than anything else, that's obvious." Her long nails bit into my wrist, but she kept on smiling. "They'll be back in a second. Don't say anything to them. Just inform me where The Piggy is!"

The front door squealed and she was back in her easy

chair, sipping her drink. I spun around. Joe stood watching us, his arms full of soggy sheets. "You two look like you've been having quite a cozy little chat," he said, water dripping down his nose.

"Poor Joe!" Zena said cheerfully. "So sad there's no extra bedding. I just *hate* to think of you sleeping on a bare mattress in this weather."

"Don't fret about me," Joe said, his eyes on her face as he wiped his nose on one of the sheets. "I'll just sleep over at Barney's. I know his parents wouldn't mind, under the circumstances."

I could tell by Zena's expression that she liked that idea about as much as I did.

"Zena, you promised you'd make the salad," Manny whined from the kitchen doorway. "And if you don't hurry up, everything's going to be *ruined.*"

Zena finished her drink and stood up. "Coming Manny," she sighed and marched to the kitchen.

Joe trudged into his bedroom, which was off the fireplace end of the living room, and dropped the sheets on the floor. He turned on the light, then pulled off his damp shirt and reached for a towel. "Hey, Barney, come on in here for a second," he said, jerking his head at me.

I obeyed. I was getting a little weary of intense confrontations, but I was curious about what impossible thing he was going to come up with. I had already been offered eternal youth and beauty, unlimited intelligence and power. What else was there?

"Did you ever think about travel, Barney?" he said, thick muscles moving on his bare chest and arms as he dried his hair.

"Mom and Dad said that *maybe* I could go to Europe

the summer after I graduate," I told him, sitting down on his stripped bed.

He tossed the towel aside. "Europe!" The way he said it, it sounded as exciting as the next suburb. He looked down at me and chuckled, his hands on his hips. It occurred to me that Mom and Dad, even together, would be no match for him. "Europe? I'm thinking about Andromeda, Barney. About Sirius, about Betelgeuse. They all have planets, *amazing* planets, believe me." He pulled a white cotton sweater out of a drawer and slipped it over his head as he talked. "I know it sounds impossible, but no more so than what the others offered you, right?"

I started to agree, then clamped my mouth shut.

"Good boy, Barney, don't expose them." He laughed nervously. "Well, whatever they may have claimed, it can't beat what I've got." He leaned against the doorway and folded his arms across his chest. "Hyperspace," he said. "Anywhere in the universe in an instant."

The whole thing was crazy. First they wouldn't tell me anything. Now they were all telling me things I couldn't believe. And I still wasn't getting any of the answers that mattered. "Just like in the game, right?" I asked him. "Does that mean the game is real?"

"Access to hyperspace is real," he said, quite seriously. "But it's going to be centuries before anybody on this planet stumbles into it. Unless you give me The Piggy."

"Prove it," I said.

He laughed again. "Good for you, Barney," he said. "Tonight's going to be very interesting."

"What do you—"

But he didn't give me a chance to ask him what he meant. "No, I can't prove anything now. I just thought I'd place an offer in advance, like the others did. And I'm not one for a lot of words, and there's no time now anyway. But the offer holds. Remember that, when the time comes. Now I want a quick drink, before we eat."

I didn't realize I was ravenous until Zena, Joe, and I sat down—I hadn't touched any of the food Mom had left me. This meal, even on the oddly assorted chipped plates, looked as luscious as the glossiest cookbook cover. Manny appeared last, flourishing a stained kitchen towel and a bottle of champagne. "It should be a noble Piper Heidsieck, but I'm afraid it's only an inane little Californian. You open it, Joe. These corks make me nervous."

Joe was as dextrous with the champagne bottle as he was with all physical things. I tried not to think about Mom and Dad as the cork exploded across the room and the wine spurted like pale blood from a sliced jugular. "I propose a toast," Zena said, raising her glass.

I lifted mine as the others did.

"To Barney," Zena said.

They all watched me.

"Why me?" I said, self-conscious.

"To give you fortune in tonight's game, Barney dear," Zena said, with her sweetest and most girlish smile.

"Hear hear!" said Manny and Joe.

They were making a very pretty ceremony of cheering me on, but I wasn't cheered. What would the game be like tonight, in the context of their outrageous offers, and my knowledge of the real thing hidden in the bookcase? The distinction between what was real and what wasn't had become disturbingly elusive. I couldn't stop wondering about Mom and Dad. And I remembered hearing somewhere that it was *not* good luck to drink a toast to oneself.

"Bottoms up!" Zena cried gaily.

"To Barney!" they all repeated in unison.

I put the wine to my lips, but I didn't touch a drop until the others had drained their glasses. And I made my own silent toast.

To The Piggy! I thought fervently, and drank.

Then the lights went out.

13

So darkness *was* necessary to their plan.

There was no moonlight coming through the windows. I could see nothing but a dull glow from the fireplace. The sound of the rain was as brittle and percussive as if marbles were being hurled onto the cottage's tin roof.

Joe found the flashlight almost at once, and soon after that a large box of candles. In minutes, the table was lit romantically, and we were all digging in as if nothing had happened. None of them seemed flustered. I thought of Manny's casual and accurate prediction about the phone going dead.

The champagne, however inane Manny considered it, tasted fine to my inexperienced palate. I had several glasses, unwisely perhaps, but it did increase my confidence. As the meal progressed, I felt more included and equal than ever in the neighbor's banter.

"I'm sorry about the beans," Manny said. "They wouldn't be so overcooked if Barney hadn't distracted me."

"I think the beans are delicious," I said, since Manny seemed to be fishing for a compliment. "Everything is wonderful." I knew it was also not poisoned. They had let me serve myself first, and I had waited for them to take their first bites before tasting mine.

"Amazing, how perceptive he turned out to be," Manny said.

"He does have a way about him," Zena agreed.

"Full of surprises," Joe mumbled, his mouth full of unpeeled new potato.

"What did you expect me to be, some dope who wouldn't wonder about you at all?" I asked them.

"Well, we weren't planning on certain unforeseen developments," Zena said.

"You should have been more careful then," I told her. I felt funny to be instructing them. "I mean, anybody could have seen that you were looking for something. And then you let me play the game, and I just put two and two together. You must have a pretty low opinion of people, if you didn't think *anybody* was going to get curious."

"Ted didn't," Zena pointed out.

"Your parents didn't," said Joe.

"For some reason, your act worked better on them than it did on me," I said.

"Act?" Zena said, in that humorous sarcastic way of hers. "Barney, you're hurting my feelings." She giggled.

"Well, whatever it was that gave Dad the nutty idea you were concerned about poverty—your disguise attribute card, or whatever you want to call it," I said, a little surprised at my own boldness. "The one that made everybody see you the way you wanted them to—except me."

"Maybe it's his *age*," Manny speculated, watching me over his glass. "He *is* the first teenager we've dealt with. Maybe they're harder to put things over on than—"

"What became of that *pie* you were talking about, Manny?" Joe interrupted him, standing up.

"Oh, that's right, the pie." The men carried plates into the dark kitchen.

"How do you know you didn't see us the way we wanted you to, Barney?" Zena asked me, staring into the candle, her hair drifting into shadow. "You still know hardly anything about us. You may be in for some surprises." Her profile hung disembodied and masklike beside the flame. "Not necessarily pleasant ones," she said softly, and turned to me. "But with the intelligence booster, at least you'd be better prepared. Safer. All you need to do is tell Zena where the little Piggy is," she coaxed me, as though she were talking to a baby or a pet. "And you can have the intelligence booster, and other gifts too. Zena knows how to express her gratitude." And she actually reached over and tickled me under the chin.

But I wasn't insulted. The wine made me feel in control. "We'll see," I said slowly, imitating her persuasive tones. "I'll think about it—*if* you're nice enough, *if* you tell me what The Piggy really does. . . ."

"But Barney, you've *played* the game," she said. Was there an edge of desperation in her voice? Did I have that much power? "Here they come! Tell me now!"

"I just hope it's had enough time to chill," Manny said, hurrying in and plunking a meringue-covered pie on the table. Manny cut the pie quickly and passed slices around. He didn't seem to have selected a special one for me. But I let the others taste it first.

It had a biting, acid flavor, not as sweet as the desserts I was used to. It cleared my head a bit—enough to remind me that however powerful I felt, I still had too many questions and hardly any answers at all. Why wouldn't they tell me what The Piggy was, and above all what it *did*? Was it really more valuable than all the incredible things they were offering me?

Then another thought struck me: Time. They tried to appear casual, but their search had not been leisurely at all. They had wasted no time since the moment of their arrival, making their moves as quickly as was possible without attracting attention. And Mom and Dad being gone, and the phone and electricity cut off—that had happened very quickly too, once they had suspected that I had The Piggy. It all *seemed* very natural. Yet no sooner had I hidden it, than I found myself in an extremely vulnerable position.

Did a real Piggy mean there was a real timer as well? A real timer that was running out?

"I just had the most *marvelous* idea!" Zena cried.

"You really don't think it was too sweet?" Manny said, tasting another dab of pie with his finger.

"What's your idea?" said Joe.

"Why don't we play tonight's game at Barney's house?" Zena looked around at the others. "For a change of ambiance. Since his parents aren't there. It's so *dreary* here."

"But they might come home and interrupt it in the middle," I said. I didn't like her idea.

"They won't go out on the road in this rain," Joe said. "If they come back at all, it won't be for hours."

"But wouldn't the board get wet, carrying it over there?" I said. I didn't want them in our house, so close to The Piggy.

"Not in a plastic bag," Zena said.

"And then we wouldn't have to clear the table," Manny said. "We could start playing right away, this minute."

"But ... but we don't have all the refreshments that you do," I argued.

"What's the matter, Barney? Don't like to think of us getting near your precious Piggy?" Zena taunted me.

"I'd think you'd *want* to be over at your house," Joe said. "They might be repairing the phone lines right now. Your parents might call."

I gave up. We stumbled over in the noisy wet darkness, following Joe with the flashlight. The old house was more of a sound than a shape, the front door banging, the windows rattling in the wind. I scraped my shins on the porch steps, behind the others. The nearer they got to The Piggy, the more uncomfortable I became. I no longer felt that I had taken it from them unfairly. It was mine now. I didn't want their hands on it. I didn't want them anywhere near it.

I could understand the way the captain's brother had felt about it, clinging to it even as he was pushed from the ship and dragged from the water. How had it gotten to the island, anyway? Had the captain decided that his brother's obsession with it was unhealthy, and taken it from him? I thought of the brother, locked in my room, watching the captain row with it out to the boulder. Was it only brain damage that had caused him to claw the walls all those years, carving the lines that pointed to the boulder? Or had the thing on the island called him?

In the hot stuffy darkness of the living room we stood grouped together as Joe flashed his pale beam around the walls. I did my best not to look at the bookcase. "The dining room table would be the best place," I said.

We lit the first candle and stuck it, with melted wax, into an ashtray shaped like the state of Florida. In the flickering dimness we set up the game. No one spoke. It was a ritual.

Again, Manny drew Moyna. Then Zena drew Zulma, which seemed an amazing coincidence. When Joe drew Jrlb, I began to be a little alarmed.

"Isn't this weird," I said. "You all drew the same ones as before."

They watched me. There were four candles now, one for each of us. The light from below made their cheekbones stand out and their eyes sink back into shadow, so that I could not read their expressions.

I drew my card. "Well at least I didn't get Luap again," I said.

Then it was as though a hand seized my throat. On the card was a drawing of me, in highly realistic detail, like an illustration from an anatomy book. Homo Sapiens were the words underneath.

"Wait a minute," I managed to say, my mouth suddenly dry. "I never saw . . . This card wasn't in the game before!"

"Look at the board, Barney," Zena said.

"But how come I never . . ."

"Look at it, Barney."

The board was easy to see in the light from the four candles. It had changed. There was a new planet, blue and green and wreathed with clouds. A planet named Earth.

It seemed impossible. Yet I could not deny what I saw on the board, or on the card in my hand. And would the new character and planet have magically appeared in the rule book too? I looked around at the silent others, my heart thudding in my ears. It was like the nightmare of finding the real Piggy, only now there would be no Mom at the door to wake me out of it.

"Welcome to the game, Barney," the others said.

138

14

"But ... but how, *why* did you do this?" I finally managed to say.

"Don't blame *us*, Barney," Zena said, shuffling cards. "*We* tried to keep you out of it. *We* tried to make you yield The Piggy before it was too late. But no; Barney's too dense to take the hint, too stubborn, too curious. *He* has to know what it's all about. *He* has to hold The Piggy, and make it a secret, and hide it from us. And once you go that far, that's all it takes. Bang! The Piggy drags another little species into the game."

"Not one that will be much of a threat to any of us," Joe said coolly.

"But it means more inferior players cluttering up the board," Zena said. "And it's so frustrating to know how long The Piggy sat here in real time without making any mischief. And then, just as I'm about to get my hands on it, this little simpleton has to stumble along and interfere. *Sapiens,* they call themselves." She made a derisive grunt.

Describe emotional response to spurious insults, recited a little mechanical voice inside my head.

I almost jumped out of my seat. I looked behind me, but there was no one. The others hadn't seemed to notice anything. Was I going nuts? Maybe the tension was pushing me over the edge.

And yet, the impossible voice made a certain sense. Their insults *were* spurious. Inferior player? Not much of a threat? "I found The Piggy first, didn't I?" I said. "Isn't *that* what counts?"

"Just look yourself up in the rule book, if you want to know what we mean by inferior, Barney," Zena said drily. "But be hasty about it."

I found the entry. I wasn't familiar enough with the book to be certain it had not been there before. But wouldn't I have noticed it?

Genus & Species: Homo sapiens

Common Name: Man

Personal Name: Barney

Sex: Male

Intelligence: IRSC 93.7

Habitat: North temperate zone
    of the planet Earth

"93.7!" I yelled. "That's ridiculous!"

"Certainly is," Manny chortled.

"But it can't be *that* bad!" I insisted.

140

"That's what we're moaning about, Barney," Zena said wearily. "It's just going to drag the game down to have more underdeveloped species like yours. Moyna's bad enough as it is."

"Now wait a minute," Manny said.

"But the game *is* real?" I said. "You really do hop around to different planets, looking for The Piggy?"

"You haven't deduced that *yet*?" Zena said, adding, to the others, "And he's shocked by his IRSC."

I refused to be baited. "Then what's *this*?" I asked, gesturing at the board. "And if you didn't want me in the real game, why did you ask me to play this one?"

"This is a . . . kind of a simulacrum," she said, as if she weren't really sure herself. "And we asked you to play because usually it works as an effective prod. A way of letting a species know the kind of danger he'll be falling into if he doesn't give us The Piggy—but without informing him directly. It was also the best way I could think of to get you so badly burned that you wouldn't be able to interfere with our island expedition."

"Only in Barney's case, neither strategy worked," Joe said.

I felt a kind of horrified awe, that she would plot deliberately to put me through so much pain. "Burns . . . burns can be really dangerous," I said stupidly.

"But nothing compared to what you're in for now," she said.

"She was trying to protect you, to keep you out; that was what it really amounted to," Manny explained. "Only your IRSC was too pitiful."

"Come, Barney, choose," Joe said. "We can't sit here explaining things all night. Are you prepared to take your equipment?" He had his hand on a pile of cards.

"But aren't you supposed to deal the attribute cards?"

Zena sighed. "This is real now, remember? So it's different from the prototype game. We already possess equipment. We brought it with us. The others did too. Now you may choose from what's available. And you only have as long as the timer allows."

"But I thought the timer was supposed to time the whole game."

"Not anymore. The Piggy will end the real game."

Joe pushed the cards at me and hit the timer. The black began moving swiftly across it.

I didn't understand much; I had more questions than ever now. Was I really supposed to accept the impossible reality of it? Would I be going to other planets? Involved in direct combat? What did she mean by "the others"? Wasn't anyone going to spell it out for me?

Apparently not. What I did know was that the right equipment was vital. Stifling my questions, I pored over the cards. My hands shook; the complex, supertechnological machinery blurred before my eyes. With my abysmal IRSC, I probably had no hope of making the right choices. And the others knew it. Zena drummed her fingernails on the tabletop, as though even giving me the chance to choose was a pointless delay.

I'm not as stupid as they think. They'll never find me here. Not as stupid as they think, came the dull, droning voice in my head again.

Again I jumped and looked around and could see nothing. I didn't *feel* crazy, so where was the voice coming from? It made me think of Luap's slug—only I wasn't Luap, and I didn't have a slug. If this kept happening, I was going to have to figure out what it meant, and fast.

142

Meanwhile, what it said seemed again to be true. I *couldn't* be as stupid as they wanted me to feel. My resolve stiffened. The cards came into focus.

There was no machine for space travel among these cards. Joe had the access to hyperspace. That meant, thinking *realistically*, that I would have to remain on Earth, where The Piggy was anyway. So I wouldn't need equipment for survival in space, or on other planets. I wouldn't need supplies of food, or heat pumps, or disguises to fool the locals.

The ocean seethed outside, closer than ever, like a hungry living organism inching toward the house. I remembered that Jrlb could breathe under water. And so I selected an oxygen-breathing apparatus that looked as though it might fit me. I discarded the rest of the travel equipment.

I took a closer look at the disguise card, before discarding it. "Disguise Selector" was what it actually said. As though you could choose to resemble whatever creature you wanted. That might be useful. I kept it.

Weapons. Those cards made me a little sick. I glanced at the timer. It was half black now. I returned to the weapons. They were mostly bombs, some that could be set like booby traps, others like missiles, others that could be thrown like hand grenades. I refused to blow anything up and thrust them aside. That left only the neural whip. I would have preferred a stunning or paralyzing gun, which seemed cleaner, less brutal. But nothing like that was available. I kept the whip.

There was an immunity card, probably for some bacteria. I didn't like the idea of disease, and kept it without looking at it.

There was lighting equipment you could wear on your head, but I discarded it, thinking of the flashlight in the kitchen. I almost kept the automatic translating headset, enabling you to understand any language. But what good would it do me? Whatever they said among themselves would be lies, since they were one another's enemies too, not just mine.

Time travel would have been wonderful, but someone else must have the Portable Access to the Fifth-Dimensional Matrix—or else Luap had lost it. Zena had the brain booster, so I'd be stuck with my own IRSC.

There were only seconds left on the timer. I had chosen just four cards. All the rest I had discarded, not wanting to be burdened by equipment I wouldn't need. Should I go back through the cards again and take back some of the weapons and equipment I had so hastily thrown away?

The buzzer went off. I was stuck with the four cards in my hand: an oxygen breather, a disguise selector, a neural whip, and the disease immunity.

"Only four cards, Barney?" Zena asked me, raising her eyebrows. "So many discards. You must be *very* confident."

I tried to think, ignoring her sarcasm. No one was going to spell things out for me—though they did seem willing to answer certain questions. But only until the game got underway. Once that happened, I was sure they wouldn't tell me anything. I had to get as much true information as I could, while I had the chance.

"What was that you said before, about the others?" I asked. "Who are the others?"

"You mean you imagined *we* were the only players, Barney?" Zena said. "Can't you get it through your little head that we've gone beyond that simple four-man plastic prototype? There are other creatures playing too. We just happen to be the first to reach this planet. But I suspect the others have arrived by now." She didn't sound very happy about it.

Manny turned and looked out the window behind him, toward the deserted beach. It was possible to distinguish wind-tossed shapes outside, blurred through the rain that streamed across the glass.

There was a thump on the front porch, and a scraping, skittering sound, like a branch in the wind. We all jumped.

"The others, perhaps," Joe said.

"Do we know how long the game is going to last?" I asked quickly.

"The Piggy knows. The Piggy decides," Manny whispered, with terrified reverence. "The Piggy ends the game. And The Piggy's been waiting for a long time now."

The three of them slowly stood up.

"But what *really* happens at the end?" I cried, jumping up and knocking over my chair. "Is *that* the same? The only survivor is the one with The Piggy, and the other players and their home planets, are destroyed?"

They watched me silently.

"But it *can't* be the same, you jerks!" I roared. "It's just too ... too huge, too awful." I couldn't find adequate words. "And it wouldn't make sense. If all the players but one were wiped out every time the game ended, how could the game go on? The game would stop! It would destroy itself the first time anyone played!"

Without speaking, they began backing away from the table, fading into the dark.

"But you *have* to tell me how it ends!" I begged them, my voice cracked and wavering with hysteria. "I'm one of the players now. Don't I *have* to know the truth?"

"We learned the game, as did you, from the board," Zena said. Only she sounded different, chittering and metallic and forced, as though the human words came unnaturally to her. "That is all we know of the ending of the game."

"But what about the last game you played?" I was close to crying now. "How did that one end?"

"Thiss iss sstill our firsst game," hissed a dark, totally unrecognizable voice. And the three of them were gone.

15

Their departure, though silent, created a disturbance in the air. Three of the candles went out.

I must have screamed. Then I was crouched over the remaining candle, whimpering, my hands cupping the flame. I couldn't think at all. My mind was a reeling mess.

I remained in that position until I felt a draft on my neck. I had the sensation of someone moving in back of me. I spun around.

No one was there. But I decided that I would be better off with something solid behind me, instead of standing defenseless in the center of a dark empty room. I pulled the candle out of the Florida-shaped ashtray and retreated from the table until I felt the wood paneling press against my back. Now, at least, I could not be attacked from behind.

They didn't know how the game ended either. This was still their first real game, however long it had been going on. Other things about the board game were different from the real one. Was the ending accurate, or would that be different too?

At least they were as ignorant as I was about the outcome. We were all in the same boat. That gave me a little comfort.

Unless they had been lying. They had never given me any reason to trust them. Maybe they *did* know the real ending, but just weren't telling me. To weaken me.

But then how could I plan a strategy? How could I do anything? It wasn't fair to be thrust into a dangerous game without knowing the rules. Panic and hysteria boiled up inside me again. I didn't have a chance.

The scrabbling sound ran across the front porch, louder now. Upstairs a door slammed, and my candle went out. I was staring directly at the blotchy, gesturing shapes outside the window. My knees collapsed. I dropped the candle and sank to the floor, blind and whimpering.

Why did you not heed me? With my knowledge, I might have prolonged his life. Speak, man. You are not deaf and dumb, the little voice woodenly suggested.

I gasped, and rolled over to protect myself from it. But, as before, there was no one there. The voice seemed to be speaking directly into my brain.

Frightened as I was, I was somehow able to think more rationally about this voice, now that the others weren't sitting there staring at me. And I realized that a voice inside my head didn't have to mean I was crazy. It could mean that someone was speaking to me through ESP—that was no more impossible than a lot of other things that had already happened.

But *who* was speaking to me? The voice hadn't started until I had drawn my own personal card and entered actively into the real game. What did that signify? And what was it Zena had said about someone dragging me into the game?

That was when the marvelous idea occurred to me. I sat up, suddenly hopeful again. Perhaps it was *The Piggy*! After all, I was the player in possession of The Piggy. Perhaps The Piggy communicated with that player during the game, and helped him.

Maybe it even answered questions. *Are you The Piggy?* I thought at it. *Is that who you are?*

Yn swlllyyybg k'sshhhhrlkthththwzzz, the voice replied, in a kind of reptilian gurgle.

"Great, that's just great," I whispered, disappointment flowing back. "And me without the translating headset."

The equipment! I had forgotten about it—until the voice, albeit indirectly, had reminded me of it. I scrambled to my feet. The equipment wouldn't be just cards now. But where was it? I'd never find it without the flashlight. And I needed the equipment now, before someone attacked. I inched along the wall toward the opening into the kitchen. I turned the corner. It was darker in here, the windows over the sink were smaller. I couldn't see, but I knew that the flashlight was usually on top of the refrigerator. My hands outstretched, I started across the room.

I stopped. What if one of them was waiting in here, between me and the flashlight? All three of them could move quietly. And they were all bigger and stronger than I was, even Manny.

Then I remembered the way their voices had changed as the game had begun. As though they had dropped their disguises and reverted to their true forms.

What if Zulma was crouched in the middle of the kitchen floor? And had I even put the flashlight back on top of the refrigerator after using it that afternoon? If it wasn't there, I'd never find it.

I listened to the rattle of the windowpanes, the unsteady drumming of the rain. And there was no rhythmical gulping hiss, the telltale sound of Zulma's ever present breathing gear. They would have to have breathing gear now, in their natural forms. That meant there was no one else in the room.

I ran for the refrigerator. I slid my hand over the smooth cold surface. My fingers closed around corrugated plastic. I grunted with relief, and with my back against the refrigerator door I switched on the flashlight.

The equipment was arranged on the kitchen table, as welcome as birthday presents shipped by UPS. I recognized the whip at once, shiny and white, coiled like a vicious albino snake. I grabbed for it, eager for the protection it offered. I stopped my hand just in time, half an inch from the bright needle at the tip. I didn't know how it worked, but it wouldn't be wise to touch the business end. The ridged handle felt like rubber and fitted easily into my hand. I stepped carefully away from the rest of the whip as I pulled it from the table. Tentatively, I gave it a feeble flick. The needle at the tip fizzled like a sparkler.

I wasn't sure I would ever be able to use it, but I stuck the handle into my belt and turned back to the other equipment. There was a brownish green capsule the size of a marble: the immunity pill. I hesitated, then gulped it down, wondering if it was the right thing to do.

Describe physiological sensation of swallowing antidote, requested the robotlike voice

It doesn't feel like anything, I answered automatically. Then I remembered my question about the voice. *Come on, just tell me the truth,* I asked it. *Are you The Piggy? Please, tell me.*

It is the Devil, the Devil, he revealed his true nature to me, Tobias. I had to do it. It is the Devil, the voice replied, emotionlessly.

I sighed with frustration. Its answers to specific questions were even less helpful than Zena's. Zena, who was really Zulma, and might attack at any minute. I had better deal with the rest of the equipment now, while I had the chance.

The underwater breathing gear was recognizable by the tube and face mask. Instead of a metal cylinder it had a kind of plastic balloon. The apparatus fit over my shoulders like a lightweight backpack. It would be no hindrance to movement. I couldn't picture exactly how I might be suddenly swept out into the water, but who knew what Joe—or Jrlb—might be able to do with the hyperspace card? It might make sense to keep the respirator on.

The disguise selector looked like a digital watch and fit snugly around my wrist. There was a blank screen and three little buttons marked ACTIVATE, DEACTIVATE, and SELECT. When I pressed SELECT, a variety of creatures flashed quickly but distinctly onto the screen. I recognized the ones from the game, including Zulma, Moyna, and Jrlb. There were others that were new to me. When I lifted my finger from SELECT, the image remained for several seconds—long enough to enable me to press ACTIVATE if I desired. DEACTIVATE would presumably bring me back to my normal appearance.

Why did it fit me so neatly, I suddenly wondered, as did

151

all the other equipment? Why were the instructions in English? And why, for that matter, had the rule book been in English, and the writing on the cards? I was baffled for a moment. Then I remembered how, when I had first looked at the rule book, the words had seemed to squirm for an instant, before becoming legible. It was understandable in the language of whoever happened to look at it. Any game played by so many different species would have to be built that way.

And when would one of these species start to do something? How much time had passed since the others had gone? I knew they wouldn't leave me in peace for much longer.

Then I heard the scrabbling sound again. Only now it wasn't on the front porch; it seemed to be coming from the dining room. Whatever was making it had crept inside and was headed for the kitchen.

Did I dare investigate it with the flashlight?

Describe physiological sensation of being on the point of immediate extinction, requested the voice.

I spun around. Jrlb stood in the center of the kitchen. It was not like looking at his picture on the card. He emitted a powerful briny reek. Salt water and scummy foam dripped from his smooth oily gray hide. He stood upright, leaning forward slightly. His hands and feet were huge and webbed and covered with scales, spread far apart to help him balance. He had no neck, or nose, or ears. Red rectangular goggles hid his eyes. His mouth was a wide lipless slit beneath the glasses, pressed tightly shut. The three foot long sword had a mean saw-toothed edge, and as he leaned forward, the barbed tip pointed directly at my eyes.

His arrival had been silent and instantaneous. He was devoid of his crippling breathing gear. With the hyperspace card he could hop instantly back to the ocean, like a swimmer coming up for air, whenever he needed a breath. And how often would that be? Certain sea creatures, I knew, could hold their breath for astonishing lengths of time.

I backed against the table, one hand on the flashlight, the other on the whip. Jrlb moved heavily toward me, swaying. His sword swung back and forth, buzzing faintly, so close that I could feel the wind of it on my face. One stroke would take off my nose, or blind me. I knew he would maim before he would kill, because he wanted The Piggy. And I could get rid of him, unharmed, without even having to use the whip. All I had to do was tell him where it was.

No. I have been there before, the voice stated dully.

And I did not want to give it up. This wasn't Joe anymore. It was a stinking fish thing that would carve me up slowly, piece by bloody piece, to get what it wanted. And The Piggy, if that's what it was, wanted *me!*

Jrlb was powerful, but clumsy out of his element. I made one small quick movement with my hand. The whip's needle sizzled against his foot. He lurched to the side. A gurgling bellow of pain escaped his lips; the reddish slits on either side of his face gaped open. He vanished, leaving behind his stench, and a puddle on the linoleum.

But he'd be back, as soon as he got another breath of water. And he could turn up anywhere, closer to me this time, slicing as he came. I pulled a chair out of the way and slid under the table.

Squatting there, I became aware again of the sound from the dining room. It was a busy lapping sound, like a multitude of mouths slithering across the floor. The kitchen floor now. It hadn't even paused during our battle. As if Jrlb's sword and my whip were irrelevant to its oozing progress.

I pointed the light at it. A flat pinkish smear, like a squashed jellyfish, extended from the dining room across several feet of kitchen floor. It was spreading. In my direction.

Salt water splashed across my face, blinding me. Something tightened around my torso, pinning my arms to my sides. The flashlight and the whip clattered to the floor as I was dragged out from under the table and jerked to my feet. I struggled, but the lasso tightened painfully around my ribs and wrists. I couldn't really see the hulking shape that held the cord, but I could smell it. Jrlb was back, and he had me bound and helpless.

He couldn't talk, holding his breath, but he didn't need to. There was a faint humming, a whisper of wind, and a razor sliced into my cheek. I screamed.

Jrlb waited, silent as a shark in a tank. Only there was no wall of glass to protect me. Instinctively I tried to reach up and wipe off the blood trickling down my face. But my hand wouldn't move. The cord tightened.

Jrlb's goggles enabled him to see in the dark—the lasso had been accurately thrown, the cut aimed precisely. It had only been a warning, inflicting no permanent damage. But he wouldn't be so kind again. Another slash might take an ear.

What do I do now? I appealed to the voice. *Help me, please!*

You must never leave this room again, Ethan. And I am only helping you by taking away this object which so obsesses—

154

Oh, be quiet! I furiously ordered it. Why couldn't it say something sensible?

The next cut went deeper, slicing through the sleeve of my T-shirt. "Stop it! Wait a second. I'll tell you!" I begged Jrlb, hoping to stall him until he ran out of breath. But maybe he wouldn't run out. Porpoises, I suddenly remembered, could hold their breath for half an hour.

Then, to my right, the basement door creaked open. I could only vaguely distinguish the squat, rounded shape at the top of the stairs. But the steady hollow throb of the breathing gear was unmistakable.

Zulma had arrived.

16

Zulma was less than four feet high, but she was so big around that she could not get through the cellar door until she crawled up on the wall and squeezed through sideways. I heard the scratch of sharp bristles on the door-frame as she dragged her bulk into the room. Against the pale shape of the refrigerator, I could see that the joints of her legs were higher than her body. The facet of an eye glimmered in the faint light from the window as she paused to survey the scene.

She spoke. It was a hoarse, guttural chirping, as jarring as the screech of an amplified needle sliding across a record, and it exploded with sudden clicks and cackles and moist sputterings. Without a headset I couldn't understand it, but it was a sound of such piercing foulness that it was probably better not to know the meaning.

Unattractive as she was, Zulma's arrival was a stroke of luck. They were enemies, not cohorts anymore. Jrlb's torture would have to stop, so that they could fight over me. In the ensuing battle, I might be able to get out of the lasso, get my equipment back, and get away from them.

Then Zulma moved toward me with unexpected speed. Why wasn't Jrlb stopping her? I tried to tell myself that she couldn't kill me, or even hurt me much, until I revealed The Piggy's hiding place. But it wasn't easy to be rational with all those legs and teeth coming at me. I went berserk, howling and fighting and screaming, too demented to tell her where The Piggy was even if she had given me the chance. I didn't go on fighting for long. In moments, I was bound like a mummy in her slimy threads, coiled into a fetal position, helpless on the floor. She kicked me out of the way, under the table again. Only then, with the prize neatly wrapped and going nowhere, did she and Jrlb square off.

He lunged with his sword. She skittered out of the way, spitting venom at his face. He lunged again, unharmed; Zulma's aim had missed. She brandished some kind of gun. Before she had a chance to use it he struck with his sword and ripped the gun from her claw.

It was a voiceless battle, but for the unvarying rhythm of her breathing apparatus. I didn't enjoy watching it. I closed my eyes. And suddenly I remembered Mom and Dad. It was getting late. Maybe they'd be home soon, in time to save me.

Save me? That was a laugh! All that would happen when they walked in the door was that they'd be killed— by one creature or another. It was just one more awful possibility that I was helpless to deal with.

But I couldn't stand being helpless. With wrenching effort I rolled over on my other side, thinking I might be able to wriggle far enough to get the whip handle in my teeth. My eyes followed the path of the flashlight beam on the maroon and gray linoleum.

Then I shrieked again. The pink smear, bubbling and spattering quietly, now covered half the kitchen floor. It was only a yard from my face.

Jrlb lurched, and his webbed foot squished down into the middle of the stuff. His bellow of agony lasted only the fraction of a second it took him to escape into hyperspace. In that short time, the puddle had been able to rip a goodly amount of scales and webbing from his foot. It ingested them rapidly, continuing its progress toward my face.

Now Zulma had seen it too. I could hear her miserable gibbering. Her claw closed around my feet and she began, haltingly, to drag me across the floor. She had won me from Jrlb, if she could get herself and me away from the stuff in time. I did what little I could to help her. I didn't like Zulma much, but the pink thing seemed to be a good deal less friendly.

Then Zulma stopped, emitting a terrible rasping wail. I twisted around enough to see that the pink thing, or its buddies, had also been coming in from the back door. We were surrounded. The cellar was now the only exit from the kitchen, and even that gap was narrowing quickly. With me slowing her down, Zulma wouldn't have time to make it to safety. She dropped me and scrambled for the cellar door. She squeezed through and clicked away down the stairs. The hiss of her breathing gear, accompanied by her frustrated twittering and whimpering, faded as she went.

I lay there as the thing spread closer. I could hear its lapping. Soon there was only an inch or so of bare linoleum around me. I waited, hardly breathing.

A narrow little finger of it oozed toward my face. It wasn't going to dissolve me all at once. It would do it bit by bit, as Jrlb had attempted, torturing me until I gave it what it wanted.

Then I remembered The Piggy. "Take it, you can have it, I'll tell you where it is!" I babbled. "Please, please. It's in the—"

But apparently it wanted to sample me anyway. The finger of pink rippled forward. It touched me on the cheek.

I closed my eyes and howled in expectation of the agony that had so terrified the others.

I stopped screaming when I realized I had felt nothing but a dry, feathery caress. I opened my eyes.

The part of it that had touched me seemed to have disintegrated. I watched as another finger reached tentatively for my nose. It withered at the touch of my skin.

Then it waited, still surrounding me. There were little indecisive ripples near the parts of it that had touched me.

It didn't hurt me the way it hurt the others. As though I were immune to it.

My 93.7 IRSC had taken awhile to realize the obvious. Perhaps it was because I had never actually *seen* the lichen before. The sapient carnivorous lichen from Mbridlengile, my character in the first game. And I was immune. That was the capsule I had taken.

Finally my brain went to work. The others didn't know I was immune. The lichen didn't realize it yet either—another finger was moving toward my chin. Sapient it might be, but it wasn't terribly bright. It seemed to take a long time for information to travel from one unit of it to the next. And perhaps I could even use it to help me, before the entire colony figured out the situation.

I gritted my teeth and rolled over on my stomach, into a solid puddle of it. It bubbled and steamed as it ate hungrily through Zulma's threads, through my clothes. But as soon as it touched my skin it withered, dry and lifeless.

In a moment I stood up. What remained of Zulma's threads and my clothes fell away from me. It didn't take the lichen long to eat off my shoes. Barefoot, I stomped gaily through it like a child playing in the rain. Under my feet, the lichen crunched like potato chips.

I still had the breathing gear and the disguise selector. The lichen had ignored the flashlight and whip under the table. I retrieved them and quickly switched off the flashlight to save the batteries. I didn't need light to ponder my next move.

I leaned back against the table. My breath gradually stopped coming in gasps. A lot had happened in the last few minutes. I was glad I had a chance to calm down a little and try to take it all in. Did the game *have* to be so violent? Or was it the nature of the players that made it so? And it moved so fast! I had been the defenseless victim of two intelligent monsters. Now, only moments later, I seemed to be safe, even in a position of power. But wasn't it just chance that had given me the lichen antidote? Where would I be now if I hadn't eaten it?

It is not only fate, my dear Ethan, but how a man responds to the blows dealt him by fate, that determines his true destiny, the computerlike voice blandly reminded me.

"That's right," I said. *I* had chosen the antidote, hadn't I? And I had been smart enough to take it while I had the opportunity.

My eyes had adjusted enough so that I could see now, without using up the flashlight—though the world was mostly shades of black and gray. Less fearful, I began moving around in the dark house. The lichen were finally beginning to get the picture, opening away from me like the Red Sea in a De Mille epic. But I didn't want it to run away. As long as it was there, the others couldn't get near me. "Nice lichen, good lichen. Just stay in the house and Barney will feed you," I coaxed it. I opened the refrigerator and tossed it a cellophane-wrapped package of bologna, to give it the idea. It gobbled it up appreciatively. I quickly closed and locked the front and back doors. Then, for good measure, I nicked a finger with a kitchen knife, and made a little barrier of blood in front of each of the doors, just in case the lichen tried to sneak out through the cracks underneath. Back in the kitchen, I tossed it the sandwiches Mom had made for me that morning, one at a time. "Do you like luncheon meat?" I asked it. "Good, isn't it? Just stay around, and there'll be more where that came from."

Zulma and Jrlb wouldn't give me any trouble for a while. I hadn't seen Moyna yet, but I knew there was very little hydrogen in the earth's atmosphere. She'd be grounded and limp, as vulnerable to the lichen as the others. All I had to do now was wait around until they gave up. I just hoped Mom and Dad wouldn't come home soon. They probably wouldn't believe whatever warnings I might have time to give them, and would be quickly eaten by the lichen.

161

Meanwhile, I seemed to have a little breathing space, and that might give me a chance to find out more about the voice.

Well, now we have some time, I thought at it with relief from the kitchen. *Who are you, anyway?*

I'm not as stupid as they think. They'll never find me here. . . . But what's wrong? Why am I losing altitude? said the voice, in its mechanical flat tones.

Now that I was a little more relaxed, the voice's non sequiturs didn't annoy me so much—they were like a puzzle, an intriguing part of the game. *But you're not losing altitude,* I soothed it, hoping to get it to say more. *You're safe down here, with me.*

Maybe Zshoozsh can help me, droned the voice. *Spiders, I need spiders. Help me, Zshoozsh! I'm going downnnnn. . . .*

Zshoozsh! That was the name of Luap's slug, who helped him in emergencies. But how could the voice be coming from Luap? He had died a hundred years ago. Nevertheless, *Are you Luap?* I asked it.

Why did you not heed me? With my knowledge, I might have prolonged his life. Speak, man. You are not deaf and dumb, recited the voice, with all the emotion of someone reading from the phone book.

I had heard that sentence before, and it wasn't Luap. It was the captain, who had said that after Luap had died. But the voice couldn't be either of those people, and it couldn't be both of them. I was beginning to feel worried again. Would I ever be able to figure it out? *Can't you just tell me if you're The Piggy or not?* I asked it.

It is the Devil, the Devil, he revealed his true nature to me, Tobias. I had to do it. It is the Devil, the voice repeated.

It was Ethan, the captain's brother who had said that! Now I was totally confused, and getting angry. *I give up! I don't care who you—*I started to say.

Then, without the aid of any artificial brain booster, I saw it. Only one entity had been with Luap in his falling ship and then with Ethan and the captain—The Piggy. Only The Piggy could have heard all the conversations it was now repeating to me.

"So you *are* The Piggy, then!" I cried out loud. "And you *are* on my side, aren't you. Come on, admit it."

Describe physiological sensation of realizing a vital truth, was all the mechanical voice would tell me.

But it was enough. "So you admit I'm right!" I shouted. "You *do* help whichever player possesses you!"

It is not only fate, my dear Ethan, but how a man responds to the blows dealt him by fate, that determines his true destiny, the voice replied.

The captain again. He had really said that, according to the document. The Piggy only seemed to report the truth. It stated things that had actually happened—the document proved that. And that meant it might tell me the truth about itself and the game—things even the others didn't know. All I had to do was ask it the right questions. And I had better do it fast. The game could change quickly.

"Okay, Mr. Piggy," I said aloud, pushing myself away from the table. "I know you only tell the truth. And now we've got some serious truth-telling to do."

"Not sso fasst, Barney," a voice whistled from above. Not The Piggy's voice. I looked up.

Moyna. In some kind of elaborate, though quiet, breathing apparatus that kept her head buoyantly fat, inflated with hydrogen. And therefore as immune to the lichen as I was. She chortled softly as she drifted toward me, stretching her talons.

17

"I'd sso been looking forward to thiss *intime* little *tête-à-tête* with you, Barney. But now it appears we are not alone, after all," said Moyna, in a mocking, sibilant whisper. "There sseemss to be a very *talkative* third party, quite closse by."

She had been hiding, listening. She had heard me exclaiming aloud about the silent thoughts from The Piggy, meant only for me. The secret thoughts that were one of my few advantages. How much had Moyna discovered from what I had given away? I grabbed the whip and the flashlight.

" 'Sso you *are* The Piggy, and you *are* on my sside,' " Moyna mimicked me, lisping. "But not on your sside for very long, I'm afraid, Barney dear." She emphasized each word with a puff of her fetid, gaseous breath.

I made the mistake of switching on the flashlight. She floated a yard from my face.

Zulma I had perceived only in darkness. Jrlb had looked like a fish, and how ugly can a fish be? But Moyna was another story. Manny's card hadn't done her justice. Her huge soft head was slimy with mucouslike membrane. Thick veins branched across it. She spasmed and pulsed like an exposed internal organ.

The long threads that undulated around her tentacles made me think of earthworms. The tentacles themselves were pliant but muscular, their undersides stippled with suction cups secreting a yellow gluey substance. The eyes above the tentacles bulged out and then retracted, and bulged again. "How about a little kiss, Barney?" she said, through the trembling, protruding mouth that made me think of a rubber balloon nozzle. And then the mouth puckered and she laughed, and the bulbous eyes swiveled alarmingly in their sockets.

But I was quick enough to see a tentacle move. I lifted the whip. Moyna sailed out of reach.

"A pretty toy, but I have my toyss too," Moyna informed me, wrapping a tentacle around a large empty cola bottle beside the sink. "And I need not hessitate in the sslightesst to make full usse of them. I do not have to be careful of you, like the otherss did. You have become disspenssable now."

"You'll never find The Piggy if you kill me," I said, hoping I was right.

"The *truth-telling* Piggy, you mean," Moyna said, with a gleeful burst of expelling gas. "The factual Piggy. Sso terribly *honesst*. Issn't that right, Barney, my friend? Cute, *sstupid* little Barney." With vicious strength she smashed the end of the bottle and brandished it like a club.

The gesture reminded me of the way Manny had brandished the rubber spatula, way back in their kitchen. But this Moyna bore no mental relationship to Manny at all. There had been a streak of kindness in Manny, a naïveté that had put him always on the verge of giving things away. This creature was even nastier, if possible, than the other two. And did she really know as much as she seemed?

"You're just putting on an act. You're not really like this," I said, trying to distract her. "You were Manny, and Manny was the *nice* one. Manny *liked* me. He wasn't like the other two. He didn't want to hurt me."

"Manny wass a better actor than the other two, that'ss all," Moyna said, taking aim with the jagged bottle. I ducked out of the way as it whizzed past my head. The force of the throw was so great that the bottle smashed against the wall behind me.

"And ssmarter, too, desspite what they may have thought," Moyna continued. The throw had flattened her somewhat against the window behind her, but now she floated forward again. "Ssmart enough to keep a transslator." (That explained why I could understand her.) "Clever enough to bide her time, to wait, to lissten, to learn."

"There's nothing to learn," I insisted, hoping my voice was steady. "You're bluffing."

"I ssusspect that The Piggy will tell the truth, to the one who possessess it. You ssaid ass much. When you die, I will possess it. Then it will tell me anything I want to know. Ssuch ass where you hid it. Ass I ssaid before, Barney, you are disspenssable now."

"No, it's not like that," I insisted. But it was too late. I had divulged enough of what The Piggy was like to give

Moyna a picture of its personality. She really believed that with me out of the way, it would tell her where I had hidden it.

Moyna was still moving toward me. I lifted the whip, sending her back across the room, toward the stove. Just in time I dodged a cast iron frying pan that she had pulled from one of the burners.

My only hope was to stay alive long enough to get more information out of The Piggy—information about what *really* happened at the end of the game, and how much time was left, and what The Piggy really was. Knowledge like that might save me, if I could get it.

A bread knife hummed past my ear, and stuck, quivering, in the wall.

The problem was, The Piggy wasn't especially terse. It didn't answer things directly. And I was not in the best situation for contemplating choice of words, or brilliant repartee.

"Thiss iss getting too tiressome for wordss!" Moyna shrilled. A tentacle reached up behind her to pull something—a weapon?—from the breathing bag fastened to her head.

I stumbled from the kitchen, my hands outstretched and groping. There was a faint rhythmic flickering on my wrist. The disguise selector! I had forgotten it.

I had only a couple of seconds before Moyna would find me and zap me. I crouched down beside the fireplace. The lichen on the hearth still hadn't learned enough to get away from me. Listening for Moyna, I pressed the SELECT button. Species flowed across the screen. Where was the one I wanted?

Moyna swept into the room, fizzling furiously. I didn't

have time to see what her gun looked like. The species I wanted appeared on the screen. I lifted my finger and pressed ACTIVATE.

The bolt from her weapon zipped past the space where my head had been, continuing on to melt one of the andirons in the fireplace. I had found my disguise just in time. Moyna squealed her frustration like a demented steam calliope. But for the moment I was safe from her.

I had become a lichen.

18

Being a lichen didn't feel at all as I would have imagined it—though, admittedly, I had never spent much time contemplating the idea.

Because it was a disguise, I did retain some of my human senses. Part of me could "see" the room, and Moyna, and the disguise selector on my wrist, and even my disguised self, like a pink soggy cornflake on the floor.

But another part of me was experiencing what it felt like to be a lichen. Not an Earth lichen, which might have been dull: a sapient, carnivorous lichen. And a special one at that, a member of an adventurous colony that was risking its life on a strange planet.

What I felt first of all was hunger. No wonder the little things were so greedy! This was like no hunger I had ever known. It was as wrenchingly persistent as the impulse to take one's next breath.

It was fortunate for Mom and Dad that the living room rug was an imitation Oriental of virgin acrylic. A real wool one wouldn't have lasted five minutes. It was also a good thing that the lichen were indifferent to linoleum, which prevented us from devouring the floors themselves.

Still, those of us in the living room weren't starving. The discomforting claim made by biologists that people live among dense swarms of invisible microorganisms—no matter how "hygienic" people imagine themselves to be—turned out to be true. There were tasty bugs everywhere, small, but in such vast numbers that we could stay alive. It was like subsisting on endless trays of hors d'oeuvres.

We lusted after the large, slimy and succulent Moyna, out of our reach for the time being. But not permanently out of reach. Only something tenuous and artificial kept her aloft. Under natural conditions she would be down here with us. And nature could often be relied upon. The main course might be coming yet.

We had followed Moyna and Zulma and Jrlb to this planet, and to this house. We wanted The Piggy too. And we had been able to recognize the creature who lived here, and who therefore must have The Piggy, by its similarity to the local organisms. We knew that eating little bits of it would quickly persuade it to give The Piggy to us—though it wouldn't have saved the creature from being rapidly devoured once we had the prize.

But now the unexpected disappointment was reaching those of us by the hearth. The creature that possessed The Piggy was poisonous. The companions who had made the first attempts at persuasion had died—as had many others upon whom the creature had inflicted itself, before the news of its nature had become widely known.

Since the individual lichen cells did not have a lot in the way of personality, losing a few dozen cells did not have the tragic impact it would have in a human population. We were not sentimental creatures; whatever "emotions" we had were limited to food. Still, companions dying was a negative experience, because it weakened us.

And now the ripples of frustration and indecision increased. The creature with The Piggy had vanished. Furthermore, we were trapped in this dwelling, by the poison it had left at the exits. There wasn't much we could do, except continue to eat. Those units directly underneath Moyna began to speculate on how it might be possible to bring her down. More sustenance would give us strength.

The Barney part of me, meanwhile, was thinking hard. I wondered at first why my touch did not wither the lichen immediately adjacent to me. It must be that, *being* a lichen, I could not be poisonous to myself, or to the others, while in disguise. That was fortunate, because it kept me an invisible member of the multitude. A single isolated lichen, with a wide swath around it, would have been an easy target for Moyna.

Continuing to eat and passing on little snippets of information were automatic functions. I seemed to be able to carry them on, while at the same time keeping my real thoughts—as Barney—to myself. The time had come for my dialogue with The Piggy. And even in disguise, I didn't have a lot of time. At any moment Moyna might get smart—or bored and impatient—and begin burning up random patches of lichen with her gun.

Piggy! I thought. *Can you hear me?*

*Describe physiological—*There was an abrupt pause. Then The Piggy whirred, *Something has altered. Describe physiological alteration.*

I'm a lichen, hiding from Moyna. But I don't have much time. The truth, Piggy! What really happens at the—

You're a lichen? That's marvelous! The Piggy's voice rose slightly in pitch, like a record played just a bit too fast. *A lichen? Oh, I envy you, enjoying such a fantastic experience. What is it like? Describe it in all possible detail!*

It's not enviable at all, I explained, trying to keep my patience. *All they care about is eating and killing. Please, there isn't much time. What are you? What happens at the end of the game?*

But I have never known the lichen experience. It is a mystery to me. Describe, describe, The Piggy begged me. *Describe each sensation of it in precise physiological detail!*

Moyna screeched again. There was a flash, and the other andiron melted. The lichen would go next.

All right, all right, I'll describe it! I frantically promised. *But first, you tell me what you are, and what happens at the end of the game!*

There was another brief pause. *Can you communicate with the lichen?* The Piggy asked me, in its original, not speeded up, voice.

Yes, yes, I'll tell you all about it. Just tell me what you are, and why all the creatures want you. Hurry!

But it is I . . . I who want them.

What?

Yes. It is I who want them. That is the function of what you call the game. Without it, I might be relegated for aeons to the depths of the interstellar void. The idea seemed to terrify it.

So the game is to make creatures want you. . . . The revelation that the game was deceptive was not a complete surprise. I had already noticed a flaw in the board game when it was translated into reality: If all the losers were destroyed, the game would end after one round. *But why is the game necessary in order to make creatures want you?* I asked. *What's so bad about you, that they would throw you away in outer space?*

I have the hiccups.

For that, I was not prepared. *But I don't get it. So what if you have the hiccups? They're harmless.*

Harmless indeed, to myself, The Piggy mechanically uttered. *An involuntary spasm, over which I have no control. Unfortunately, its effect in this universe is equivalent to a 100 megaton nuclear explosion.*

It was a good thing lichen weren't emotional. I was able to remain somewhat rational as this piece of information sank in. But the shock of it forced me to break my electrical contact with the adjacent lichen. It took all my concentration to absorb it fully, to take the statement to its logical conclusion.

That means . . . the game is backwards? I asked, after a pause. *Everybody thinks The Piggy means safety, but what really happens is, the player who has The Piggy is destroyed at the end? Not the others?*

An unfortunate deception. But circumstances gave me no other choice. Who would want me if they knew?

The adjacent lichen were beginning to notice something was wrong, bombarding me with impulses that were increasingly difficult to ignore. There was also Moyna, who would soon be taking aim at the hearth. Only my phlegmatic lichen personality kept me cool enough to inquire, *And when is your next hiccup going to happen?*

By my standards, instantly. By yours ... approximately thirty-three minutes.

19

The observer part of me glanced at the luminous dial of my wristwatch. It was 1:27.

Doing my lichen's best to remain imperturbable, I considered my options.

My first impulse was to throw off my diguise and hand The Piggy over to Moyna, who would then depart with it from the earth as quickly as her ship would take her.

But I stopped myself in time. She would shoot me as soon as I resumed my human form. And if she didn't she would be immediately suspicious. How could I explain giving up The Piggy, without giving away its secret? The only way to get rid of it was to be as indirect, and deceptive, as the game itself.

It occurred to me briefly to be noble, to sacrifice my life to save the earth by allowing Moyna to kill me and find The Piggy herself. But I quickly assured myself that without my help she wouldn't have time to find The Piggy before it went off.

I also wondered, for a moment, what would happen if Mom and Dad showed up *now*. I could hardly picture the scene. It was too terrible to contemplate.

The lichen around me were getting extremely suspicious. In a moment they would see through my disguise. I opened myself up to them. Lots of information poured in. A large arm of us, it seemed, was silently climbing the wall behind Moyna, planning to drop down upon her from the ceiling, eat through her gas bag and send her to the floor—if she didn't notice and kill us first.

But I didn't want Moyna to die. I wanted her to find The Piggy. And the knowledge that the lichen were capable of scaling vertical heights gave me an idea. Perhaps they could lead her to it.

As quickly as I could I began broadcasting The Piggy's location. The ones next to me didn't seem to understand at first. I continued sending out the information that the prize was nearby, in the bookcase directly above us. Finally my neighbors caught on. Growing as agitated as lichen can be, they began transferring the information.

It did not occur to me, at that moment, to wonder how much I could really trust The Piggy.

I sensed ripples of excitement flowing across the living room and into the kitchen. The arm reaching up behind Moyna paused. I began suggesting that we should form an arm to scale the bookcase and get the prize. Such mass movement couldn't be organized by one cell, of course. It would have to be by common consensus, which took a little while. I urged them to hurry. We had thirty minutes left.

It was out of my control now. I had given the lichen the

information; they had accepted it. I could only wait, and broadcast urgency, and hope it all went fast enough to get The Piggy out in space before it hiccuped.

Waiting around wasn't good for my state of mind. That was when I saw that there was a flaw in The Piggy's version of the game, too—a big fat one. As soon as it hiccuped, destroying the unfortunate winner of the game, and whatever planet he or she was on, The Piggy's secret would be out. The surviving players would realize at once that The Piggy was a liability, not the asset it was in the board game. No one would want it then. They would shun it. It would be relegated to an eternity in the void— which was exactly what it didn't want.

Had The Piggy lied to me?

The lichen had made a decision. I began moving along with the flow, across the hearth, toward the bookcase. Ahead of me, lichen were oozing up onto the first shelf.

But the arm on the wall behind Moyna was moving too. It had reached the ceiling and was inching along toward her head. And Moyna hadn't noticed. She was watching those of us climbing the bookcase. We were a diversion, attracting her attention and keeping her in one place until the others could reach her and fall upon her.

I was still debating with myself about The Piggy, trying to decide between the conflicting versions of the game. Which one made more sense?

Are you really telling me the truth, Piggy? I demanded. *A lot of lives depend on it.*

I'm not as stupid as they think. They'll never find me here, The Piggy blandly recited.

Forget Luap and listen to me! I ordered it. *Your version of the game doesn't work either. Help me, please! What do you really do?*

It is not only fate, my dear Ethan, but how a man responds to the blows dealt him by fate, that determines his true destiny, droned The Piggy.

Stop quoting that dumb old captain! I screamed silently, so beside myself that the lichen around me were a little startled. But I was beyond logic. *Just tell me what you really are, and what's really going to happen in twenty-seven minutes. Please, what is the truth?*

Beauty Is Truth, Truth Beauty—That Is All Ye Know on Earth and All Ye Need To Know, it said mildly. *Future Teachers of America, 2, 3, President 4; Pep Club, 1, 2; Prom Queen Attendant, 4.*

Had the thing gone mad? *Piggy, please don't desert me now!*

A Man of Honesty He Is, and Trust. Varsity Wrestling, 3, 4; Intramural Football, 3, 4; Stamp Club, 1.

But it had deserted me. It was quoting from the yearbook. True or false, it seemed to have said all it was going to say on the subject. I was on my own now.

But not really. I was still a part of the lichen colony, in the vanguard, in fact, of the arm climbing toward The Piggy We were at the level of the mantel now, mounting steadily over the tattered bindings. The observing part of me could see that the other arm had just about reached the spot on the ceiling directly over Moyna's soft throbbing inflated head. Several inches of lichen seemed to be loosening, preparing to attack.

Then, unaware of her own danger, Moyna wafted toward the bookcase, fascinated by our arm. Behind her, a dozen or so lichen tumbled silently to the floor, just missing her The arm on the ceiling began crawling forward again

I was locked into the chain of events I had begun when

179

I had wanted to get rid of The Piggy. I could do little to change anything now—which was just as well, because I was a confused wreck. I didn't know *what* to believe.

In only a few minutes, the lichen would reach The Piggy. And then, if Moyna was still alive, the battle for it would begin. When that happened, I would have to take specific action. And that action would depend on the answer to one simple question.

Did I want The Piggy or not?

20

I appealed to The Piggy again as we inched toward the ceiling, sustaining ourselves on bookworms and silverfish and mildew. The Piggy responded with more inanities from the yearbook, in its mechanical voice.

Moyna was so close to us now that her fetid succulence was intoxicating, almost overwhelming. If she had been a couple of inches nearer, we might have lost control and hurled ourselves upon her from the bookcase. But Moyna, who seemed to be familiar with the lichen, kept just out of our jumping range in this planet's gravity. We gritted our figurative communal teeth and moved up to the top shelf.

The Piggy, inside the yearbook, was quoting from the yearbook now. Before, it had quoted Luap, and Ethan, and the captain.

We were moving horizontally across the shelf toward

the yearbook. I had managed to work my way into the front line. I tried to move as slowly as possible, to give myself more time to think. "Slowly, slowly, wait, she'll take it from us if she sees," I told the others, hoping to get them to stop. It seemed to work. As the message passed to those behind us, the arm slowed. We came to a standstill several volumes away from the yearbook. The Piggy was still quoting from it.

I had thought, at first, that The Piggy told the truth. But I had been wrong. What it actually did, most of the time, was listen and quote. It didn't really communicate; it requested information and it repeated. It repeated things it read; it repeated what people said. It heard and then played back. That made me think of something—something familiar. And I was suddenly so excited that it was almost more than my lichen membranes could take.

What The Piggy reminded me of was a tape recorder. An intelligent tape recorder, that was always prompting me to describe my sensations to it.

I struggled to keep my agitation in check. But maybe I *did* have the answer. It was a kind of sentient recording device, programmed to learn—about many different species.

The Piggy certainly sounded like a machine. I tried to remember everything it had said. The only time it hadn't quoted, or prompted, was when it gushed rapidly about wanting to be a lichen. And right after that it told me that it was going to blow up. And I had immediately told the lichen where I had hidden it. Perhaps that's what The Piggy had *wanted* me to do—so that it could move on to a new species.

I felt myself being pushed forward from behind. "The

other arm is above her now. They are about to drop. Move for The Piggy. She will be eaten before she can take it from us. Move on, move on, move on."

It was like being dragged down by an undertow, or caught in a mob. The force was irresistible. We crawled along the shelf. We reached the yearbook.

Moyna's shriek was so piercing and high-pitched, it might have broken my eardrums, if I'd had eardrums. As lichen, we couldn't exactly hear, but we were keenly aware of Moyna's situation. The attack had begun.

The platoon had landed on Moyna's portable breathing bag, not her actual flesh. Though the bag was inedible, the lichen were able to puncture it instantly, rendering it useless.

With a lash of a tentacle Moyna flung the bag away from her. It careened madly around the room, spitting hydrogen, until it finally drifted to the floor, with its clinging passengers. If only one of them had achieved a landing on Moyna's actual flesh, it could have eaten through her natural gas bag, mortally wounding her and sending her down to be agonizingly dined upon.

But Moyna had moved too quickly. Not a single lichen had touched her. There was still a cubic foot of hydrogen in her head, diminishing with every breath, but still enough to keep her aloft for a short time. And that might be all she needed.

We had eaten through the yearbook cover by now, doing our best not to taste the disgusting material, ingesting and excreting it as rapidly as possible. It would be clear to Moyna that The Piggy was within the volume. But she couldn't take it from us. We swarmed all over it; one touch of her talon, and we'd be swarming all over her.

All she could do was watch and wait, tensed to pounce for The Piggy if the opportunity presented itself. But she was losing hydrogen, sinking millimeter by inevitable millimeter toward the floor, where our companions were hungrily waiting.

I ingested and regurgitated on the front line, wanting to reach The Piggy before any of the others. But I was still thinking faster than ever.

The idea that The Piggy was a recording device made more sense than anything I had come up with yet. It needed the game because its function was to learn about the players. And to record what it learned.

I ate through the last sheet of paper, and there was The Piggy, startling me again with its primitive vapid ugliness. But I knew that it was not primitive at all. I wrapped my lichen body around it, being sure to stifle all digestive functions so that it would not be harmed.

The Piggy was programmed to learn. To do so, it had to provide some reason for the subjects of its study to want it around. Otherwise, it would be neglected, empty, learning nothing. And what better reason for wanting it was there than fear—fear of being destroyed, and the resulting need for safety, for protection?

The game threatened to destroy the creatures, and The Piggy promised safety. And that was why all the creatures wanted it, and fought over it, and gave it the exciting contact with them that it craved.

But did the danger even have to be real? I wondered. Did species really have to be wiped out? Or could it be a false threat, to make the creatures compete for the protection offered by The Piggy? After all, it was what the creatures *believed* about The Piggy that would make them do what it wanted, whether it was true or not. The board game, and the awesome powers provided by the real equipment, seemed to do a good job of convincing them.

Would it be necessary for planets to be destroyed? Maybe an occasional example would be enough. Maybe just one at the beginning.

Or maybe none at all.

I had believed. Jrlb and Zulma and Moyna had believed—and none of us had known the real game to come to any conclusion at all.

But I still needed one more piece of evidence.

I was squished in the middle of a three-inch ball of lichen that had formed around The Piggy. I was also aware that Moyna had sunk several feet. Her talon, according to those waiting impatiently beneath it, was now only .734 meters from the floor.

"Hey, could I ask you a question?" I said to the lichen cell beside me. "Something I don't understand. I'm kind of new and young."

"You don't look it," my companion said.

I remembered that lichen couldn't lie to each other. "I know this Piggy thing is the prize in the game we're playing. But why do we want it, exactly? What does it do?"

"What does it do?" The lichen seemed to find the question meaningless. "It is the prize. Without it, we will lose."

"But what *happens* if we lose?"

"How did you get into this colony anyway?" the lichen asked me suspiciously. "Why are you asking these stupid questions? You seem peculiar, different. I'm not sure I like being next to you."

"Just answer me or I'll *eat* this thing!" I threatened it—I was right on top of The Piggy. "What happens if we lose?"

Now the lichen seemed frightened of me. It knew I couldn't lie, so it believed my threat. "If we lose, we will be destroyed when the game ends. Everyone knows *that*. And don't you dare eat it! We've never been this close to winning before. You'll ruin everything!"

"But what happened at the end of the last game?" I demanded. "Who was playing? Who was destroyed?"

"The last game? But this is still our first game," the lichen said. "Excuse me." It jostled the cell on the other side of it. "Could you just trade places with me? I need a change of position. I'm a little cramped over here."

I had offended it. It would probably start telling the others there was something wrong with me, and blow my disguise. But for the moment, I had learned enough from it. It had told me the same thing the other players had. It didn't know what happened at the end of the last game. Because this was its first game.

The other players could have been lying, but not the lichen. Lichen couldn't lie. None of them had actually *known* The Piggy to destroy a species, or a planet, or anything at all.

Was it really possible that The Piggy never destroyed anything? That the game was a hoax, devised to keep The Piggy in the center of the action, recording away?

It seemed too good to be true. Yet it was far easier to believe than either flawed version of the game. And if it was true, all I had to do was let the creatures take The Piggy. And I'd be safe from them, and from their brutal game.

But did I dare to believe it?

The ball of lichen around The Piggy, now six inches thick, rolled off the shelf. We squelched softly down upon a cushion of our companions on the floor. We began rippling quickly toward the front door, ignoring even Moyna, who was crumpling down beside the fireplace.

I opened myself up to the latest news. Lichen had been testing the poison at the exits. It had lost its effect. The door was locked, but busy cells had already eaten a large enough hole in the wood to get The Piggy out. And then we could be beamed with it, back to our ship.

My blood was no longer poisonous. That must mean that I, in my natural form, was no longer immune—the pill had worn off. But I was in the very center of the colony now, still beside The Piggy. If I wanted to become Barney, before getting beamed up to their ship, I'd have to work my way back to the edge, quickly.

But I had one more question for The Piggy. *Piggy, what you said about the hiccup in fifteen minutes. Why did you tell me that? Because you'd been on the earth long enough, and wanted me to let you go? Or was it true?*

There was no response.

The lichen had The Piggy now, not Barney. I was out of communication with it. It was tired of human beings, and wanted to stay with the lichen—it had told me it had never experienced them before.

And then it had told me about its hiccup. That information made me give it to the lichen. That was probably exactly *why* it had told me it was going to hiccup. And it had worked.

I had made my decision. I was moving away from The Piggy. Soon I reached a position where the mass was only one lichen thick. Then things became very difficult. The mass was moving with all its combined force toward the door. But I wanted to stay inside, to escape out of the mass. I was trying to move against the surging mob now, and it was nearly impossible. The best I could do was try to stay in one place, and not get pulled out the door with all the rest.

It would have been easy if I were still immune. But apparently I wasn't. I couldn't risk becoming Barney until I had worked my way clear of them. I did the lichen equivalent of elbowing and kicking as they swarmed past me, cursing me, furious and uncomprehending.

The decision was now irrevocable. I had sacrificed The Piggy to the lichen. If the board game was right, Moyna, Zulma, Jrlb, and Barney—as well as our planets and species—would be obliterated in thirteen and a half minutes. Only the lichen would survive.

If The Piggy was right, then the lichen ship would be inflicted with a 100 megaton nuclear explosion in thirteen and a half minutes. Who else would feel the blast would depend on how close they were to the ship, and how fast it could move. There was a good chance it would be far enough away from the earth not to do much damage.

And if *I* was right, no one would be destroyed in thirteen and a half minutes.

I hoped I was right.

21

The lichen were moving very quickly, desperate to get the entire colony out under the sky where they could be beamed with The Piggy to their ship. Despite my furious efforts at resistance, I was being dragged toward the door. If I ended up on their ship, I'd never be able to take off the disguise, or they'd eat me. I would have to remain a lichen forever.

That thought helped me to sustain my efforts. But by the time I had reached the back edge of the lichen mass, we were almost at the doorstep. And there was a wall at the back edge of the mass, a membranous skin that, as a lichen, I could not penetrate.

All around me lichen were sliding under the crack below the door. I resisted, feeling the membrane stretch like elastic. But it wasn't going to break. In another instant I would be pulled through.

Even losing a foot would be preferable to being trapped on their ship. As the observing part of me touched DEACTIVATE, the lichen part made one last push away from the door.

And then I was Barney, toppling into the living room, my bare feet on the raised threshold of the front door. I bellowed. The parting gesture of my former companions was to eat through both my big toenails. But they had no time to finish the meal, and oozed off into the night.

The pain, and the sudden disorienting change, left me stunned. I remained sprawled on the floor by the still locked front door, not thinking, feeling relief at having escaped the lichen so easily.

Then I saw Moyna—or rather her four muscular tentacles. She had dropped the gun and was dragging her deflated head toward me, pulling herself along by digging her talons into the floor.

I yelped and jumped to my feet, limping out of her way. But it wasn't me she was after now. Sure, if she'd been able to use the gun she probably would have killed me, just for the heck of it. But she was obviously too weak from lack of hydrogen to wield the gun, or do anything but drag herself painfully toward the door. All she wanted now was to get outside. Apparently, like the lichen, she needed to be in the open air in order to beam herself back to her ship.

If she didn't die first. Her veiny, wrinkled head was as flat as a cartoon character run over by a steamroller, a two-dimensional pancake. She seemed to have barely a cubic centimeter of hydrogen left. If she died, I'd have her corpse on my hands.

Quickly I unlocked the door, flung it open, and peered

outside. There was no sign of the lichen. They had departed quickly with their prize. "Come on, Moyna, out you go," I urged her. "Atta girl, you can do it, I know you can."

But she still had several feet to cover, and she could barely move at all now. Swallowing my disgust, I reached under her slippery head and draped it over my arms. It was like picking up entrails. Carefully, carefully, I carried her outside and deposited her gently on the ground at the bottom of the porch steps. She had enough energy to carve a wicked gash in my arm with a talon before vanishing.

"Gee, thanks a lot!" I shouted at the empty space where she had been. "After I help you and—"

Then I remembered the others. Jrlb, who must have been observing from some safe vantage point, would probably have reached his ship already. But Zulma would be on her way out of the house any second now. And she wouldn't be weak and harmless like Moyna. She'd want to get in her parting shot. I ran from the steps and crouched down behind a pillar of the porch.

With a throaty hiss and a brittle clatter, Zulma scurried from the house. She paused at the bottom of the porch steps. The weather had cleared. In the moonlight I saw her hideousness—the powerful jointed legs, the swollen belly, the huge insect eyes. Her bristly head swiveled like an owl's. She screeched, displaying her curving fangs.

I had been watching from almost the same hiding place when she had made her original appearance. How compelling and attractive she had been, tossing back her luxuriant hair, greeting Ted so demurely. She had drawn and fascinated me from that first moment.

Now she made one last disappointed vengeful shriek

191

and vanished as Moyna had. She would have enjoyed killing me, but she didn't have time for that luxury. She was behind the others now.

I still seemed to be wearing my old wristwatch. It was three minutes to two.

If the earth did continue to exist, I would have a long night ahead of me. The house was a mess: furniture overturned, light fixtures broken, kitchen equipment sticking into walls. And there were dead lichen everywhere, which would have to be gathered up, somehow, in the dark, and dispensed with. They would probably make excellent compost.

Now that the rain had stopped, Mom and Dad would probably be home soon—it must have been the rain that fortunately had prevented them from coming home any earlier. It would be nice to get the mess cleaned up before they arrived, to avoid trying to explain it to them.

But I didn't have to start just yet—there was no point in cleaning up if the world was going to be destroyed in two minutes. I stood up and walked to the middle of the front yard and looked up at the night sky. It was familiar, and, I suppose, beautiful. I had been in the dark for so long that the stars shone forth with unusual clarity.

They were dim and dull compared to the stars on the board. And there were no colorful, detailed planets. I had halfway expected some shooting stars, but there weren't any.

I stood and watched as the numbers on my digital watch blinked toward two o'clock.

The moment came and passed. The earth remained. There was no bright flash of a hiccuping Piggy. I waited another minute, two more minutes, just in case my watch was slow. By ten after two, still nothing had happened.

I turned back to the house.

It was going to take me a little while to adjust to the fact that it was all over now, that things would go back to normal. There was a lot I wasn't sure about, including my own interpretation of The Piggy.

But it had happened all right—the onerous cleanup that now confronted me was testimony to that. The reality of the job almost made me wish the whole thing had been a dream—almost, but not quite.

One thing I was very sure of was that I was glad it was over. The others were so vicious that they made even the human race look good. But I almost felt sorry for them now, trapped in their frantic perilous game. Maybe they enjoyed it, but they were still the dupes of The Piggy, they were still its slaves. Only I had managed to escape.

It made me wonder about their interpretation of the IRSC. Maybe they had it backward, and the higher numbers *were* better after all.

It was a satisfying thought. Broom in hand, I began to whistle. There was a lot of sand mixed in with the dead lichen. It was always that way at the beach—no way to keep the sand out.

EPILOGUE

"That pathetic, vacuous little cretin!" Zulma shrieked, her legs whirling around her wildly as she punched control buttons. "Losing The Piggy to those accursed lichen!"

"Vacuouss indeed," lisped Moyna from her own speeding ship—the three of them were communicating from their separate ships by radio. "Hiss brain musst be even more primitive than hiss IRSC ssuggesstss. He could eassily have killed me, but he wass too pitiably densse."

"We're the ones who should be blaming him for that oversight, Moyna dear, not you," Jrlb pointed out. His ship was the closest to the lichen's. "If only he'd been a little smarter, he could have put you out of the game for good—and saved us the job."

"It's just plain incomprehensible, *baffling*." Zulma had her ship on course now. She waddled from the controls and sank into her lounging net. She was not weightless; she was heavier than she was on most planets, in fact, because her ship was accelerating. "I will never understand it, never. Failing to exhibit the natural response to destroy an enemy. That species must be some kind of evolutionary blunder, a biological *lapse*. Unfit for the privilege of the game." She sank deeper, the net groaned under her weight as the ship's velocity increased.

"Fortunately The Piggy iss now out of itss handss, and we will no longer have to ssuffer that sspeciess' detesstable pressence," said Moyna. She undulated comfortably in the vat of mucus that protected her fragile membranes from the rigors of high speed travel.

"And we must make sure that some other second-rater like Luap does not drop it there again," Zulma insisted venomously. "I can only hope that the torment of his blood boiling was extreme. And to lose The Piggy in the past, on top of it all. Making it necessary for us to spend all that time in those odious disguises on that putrid planet, doing research on their rudimentary little culture in order to find it. Forcing us to work *together!*" The spinnerets on her abdomen shuddered at the very thought of that.

"We sshould have killed him insstantly, and hiss parentss ass well, ass ssoon ass we learned he had The Piggy," Moyna whined. "Then the lichen wouldn't have it now." The lichen were going to be something of a problem.

"To kill the whole family, and then be vulnerable to detection, without knowing where he had hidden The Piggy?" Jrlb paused to slurp down one of the eels that lived in his water tank. There weren't many adult eels left—he hoped the maturing eggs would hatch soon. "Even three little killings would have been noticed quickly—that species has a peculiarly hysterical attitude toward death. No, Moyna, the only way was to do as we did, and let him lead us to it."

"But to let him forfeit it to the lichen!" Their contact with one another was growing fainter as they approached light speed, but the piercing frequency of Moyna's wail made it clearly audible to the others. They had passed the orbit of Pluto. The stars were beginning to blur. "Thosse abominable lichen. Who can't be approached. Who can hardly even think. Who can predict what they will do with it? How can it be wressted from them?"

"Oh, so you don't have a strategy, Moyna dear?" Zulma's cackle was fading. "That is valuable information for me. I can make use of it in my own strategies." She paused, and her voice took on a mournful tone. "I only wish there had been time to rend the Barney creature slowly. The frustration of it leaves me empty and wanting."

"Look on the bright side," Jrlb gurgled distantly. "His species was drawn into the game. The Piggy will destroy that species at the conclusion of the game. Let us all be thankful for that."

The others agreed silently. Their ships, programmed to follow the lichen, achieved the wave frequency of light, cutting them off from one another.

The lichen ship, meanwhile, was heading for home. Its controls were operated by the lichen's slaves, a simian species, docile and small-brained, who responded well to pain. The lichen were nestled together with The Piggy on their traveling bed of rich slime mold. The bed was constantly replenished by an automatic system connected to a vast store of freeze-dried mold spores, which took up much of the space of the ship. The lichen were free to occupy themselves as they wished. Like any species in possession of The Piggy, they were attempting to learn from it.

They asked it many questions. "What can we do to keep you happy and satisfied?" "What type of organism do you take most pleasure in devouring?" "What is the secret of winning the game?"

The Student Council this year has been extremely active in school affairs and in stimulating school spirit among the student body, The Piggy whirred blandly at them.

The lichen were confused.